Murder Most Unfortunate

Books by David P. Wagner

The Rick Montoya Italian Mysteries
Cold Tuscan Stone
Death in the Dolomites
Murder Most Unfortunate

Murder Most Unfortunate

A Rick Montoya Italian Mystery

David P. Wagner

Poisoned Pen Press

Copyright © 2015 by David P. Wagner

First Edition 2015

10 9 8 7 6 5 4 3 2 1

Library of Congress Catalog Card Number: 2015932054

ISBN: 9781464204340   Hardcover
        9781464204364   Trade Paperback

Poisoned Pen Press
6962 E. First Ave., Ste. 103
Scottsdale, AZ 85251
www.poisonedpenpress.com
info@poisonedpenpress.com

Printed in the United States of America

This book is dedicated, with fond appreciation, to my Italian colleagues at the American Consulate in Milan and the Embassy in Rome, as well as to many other Italian friends from the nine years I lived and worked in Italy. It was kind of you to teach me so much about your wonderful country. *Grazie Mille.*

Chapter One

Professor Lorenzo Fortuna had been amused by the request, but not surprised. He was, after all, the most prominent scholar at the seminar. He knew the period better than all of the so-called experts who had sat at the speakers' table with him, people whose puffery and inflated rhetoric exposed rather than hid their appalling lack of scholarship. Why had he even come? Certainly not to mix with those buffoons. No, it was for the young people who formed the majority of the audience, that next generation of art historians who were attracted to him like prospective apprentices to an old master. He smiled as he thought of them. They had hung on his every word, as his students did in his own classes, enjoying when he pointed out some absurdity uttered by the other panelists.

But there were other aspects of the previous few days that had made it worthwhile. He had been put up in a comfortable hotel, the meals had been good, and the wine excellent. As was the cognac which sloshed in the bowl of his snifter now as he walked. He may have had a bit too much to drink, but it was the last night, after all, and the fellow had insisted. One should not be ungrateful for such generosity, even if it was his due. He slowed his unsteady steps in order to take another sip of the amber liquid. It burned as it went down, in a smoother and more pleasing burn than the famous local grappa that had capped every meal during the seminar.

"Here we are," said the man Fortuna was following. Unlocking the door, he reached in to switch on a large overhead fixture. Light bounced off the objects in the room. Fortuna closed his eyes tightly and then opened them wide to focus on two paintings that leaned against the wall on the top shelf of a low bookcase. There might have been other works of art in the room, but he knew immediately that these were the two he was meant to see.

He frowned. It was not the frown of disgusted annoyance, like those aimed at his fellow scholars during the seminar, but instead an indication of serious concentration. The learned Professor Fortuna getting down to business. He brushed past the other man, reluctantly put his drink on the shelf, and leaned toward the first of the two works.

"Beautiful, is it not?"

Fortuna did not reply for several minutes. "The subject…it would be his early period." He reached forward, took the painting by its frame, and adjusted the angle to take better advantage of the light.

"I can get a lamp."

"No need, I can see it well enough." He looked for a few moments longer before moving his attention to the second work. After some minutes he remembered his drink, took a taste before again setting it down, and stepped back to observe the two from a distance of about five feet. He slowly shook his head and smiled while the second man—who could hardly contain his pleasure—watched him. Fontana then pulled out a thimble-sized instrument from the vest pocket of his three-piece tailored suit. He held it to one eye and moved it around the second painting, not more than two inches from the crusted brush marks. He did the same with the first work before slipping the magnifier back into his pocket and stepping back.

"Magnificent, are they not?" Pride showed in the host's face and voice.

Fortuna took his eyes from the paintings, retrieved his snifter, and turned to the other man. "They are fakes. Well done, perhaps the best I've seen, but fakes nonetheless."

"That's impossible." The man choked on his words. "You must be joking."

Fortuna grunted. "I would never joke about such things." He tilted his head as he surveyed the two compositions. "The treatment of the faces is good, but not close to the level of other works by the artist. I might say the supposed artist. You see the arrangement of the figures? Very much out of character. He would never seat the Madonna in that position. The signature is close but not close enough. The final indication is in the brushstrokes. He never used that heavy impasto. Never." He took another sip and smirked. "Extremely well done. The painter had—or should I say has?—real skill. It certainly would fool most of the participants in the seminar, but I have a better trained eye than any one of them. I must say, these two works could not have been more fake if they had been painted on black velvet." He chuckled at his own humor.

The other man stared at the two paintings, his breaths coming rapidly. "But…you can't just…there must be some mistake."

"No mistake, my dear man. But on the plus side, I now have another anecdote to add to my lectures, so my students will be grateful to you. As I am grateful for this excellent cognac." He held the snifter up to the light and watched the contents create a shimmering, nut brown prism.

Some time later, in silence, the host inspected his two precious works, running twitching fingers over the paint and gazing so intently he nearly lost his balance. How could that arrogant bastard be right? He exhaled a long, shuddering breath and shifted his eyes from the paintings to the floor beside him. Cognac was spreading over the tiles and through the pieces of broken crystal, to mix with the darker liquid that had gushed from Fortuna's chest.

Chapter Two

Bassano del Grappa could not decide if it was going to slip into spring or keep the winter a while longer. Snow still crowned Monte Grappa as well as lower peaks which stood vigil above the northern side of the city. To the south, where the hills began to flatten into the Po Valley, green shoots were starting to break through the brown earth. The Brenta River flowed roughly past the town and under the bridge, its waters swollen as the snow receded up the sides of the lower hills. It would be ice cold, but it was always ice cold this close to the mountains. Only downstream, when it went around Padova, would it warm, and then only in the summer.

Rick Montoya stopped in the middle of the covered bridge and peered over the railing at the rushing water. He knew from previous mornings that he needed a breather before attacking the steep hill that led up through the center of the town to his hotel. And as on those other mornings, today he had passed only a few people as he jogged through the streets of Bassano. A street cleaner, the only other person on the bridge, brushed up papers and other traces of the previous evening's foot traffic. As the city's major attraction, the Ponte degli Alpini attracted more than its share of tourists. With them came the inevitable trash, even though the majority of the foreigners were fastidious Teutons.

Rick turned his attention to the mountains and thought about any similarity between the city's geography and that of Albuquerque, where he had spent so many years. OK, both were built in the shadow of mountains, but it stopped there. Northern Italy was not the high desert, the Brenta was not the Rio Grande, and the people of the Veneto were very different from New Mexicans.

He bent down to tie his running shoe. It didn't need tying, but it was an acceptable way to put off the climb facing him at the end of the bridge. After wiping his forehead with the sleeve of his sweatshirt and bouncing a few times on his toes, he was once again off. Leaving the protection of the roof of the bridge, he was once more under the open sky and starting up the hill toward the town center. He had found the name of this street, Via Gamba, amusing, given its sharp incline. He assumed that the Gamba in this case was some former resident of note and did not mean "leg," despite the ache in his own legs at the moment.

After the initial climb the street leveled off and he turned right to jog through the first of three small connected squares. The absence of cars allowed him to stride diagonally through the middle of Piazza Monte Vecchio and into the next, Piazza Libertá. Metal grating guarded the shops lining this square; it would be a few hours before the owners arrived to roll them up. The San Francesco church covered most of one side of the final square, Piazza Garibaldi. Rick wondered if there was a law requiring every town in Italy, regardless of size, to have some street, square, or park named for the most famous soldier of the *Risorgimento*. Behind the church was a former convent that now housed the Museo Civico where Rick had worked as an interpreter the previous several days.

It had been a good gig. He'd learned a lot about artist Jacopo Bassano, the city's most famous native son; he'd had some stimulating conversations with the participants at meal times; and once again he had been fascinated by the pettiness of academia. Had it been that bad at UNM? He considered that question as he reached the tree-lined street that ran along the remaining portions of the city's east wall. It bore the name Via delle Fosse, a reminder of the moat that had once run along the outside of the wall as a further deterrent to prospective invaders. As if the tall ramparts were not enough. He stretched his pace for the last hundred meters before slowing to cross the street to his hotel.

Rick walked through the lobby to receive his room key from the desk clerk. Turning toward the elevator he noticed two men sitting in one corner of the room, deep in conversation. He recalled the backgrounds of the two men and decided that scholarship did not just generate fierce rivalries, it also made strange friendships. Karl Muller, from Bavaria, was one of Germany's most prominent scholars of Italian art. He was dressed formally for the early hour, in a tweed suit, his open collar filled with a paisley ascot. All he lacked, Rick thought, was a monocle and a swagger stick. Across from Muller sat George Oglesby, who taught at a British university which Rick first heard mentioned when he'd met the man. Oglesby looked more like an artist than the art professor he was. The collar of his turtleneck shirt hung loosely, despite the size of the man's neck, and his trousers looked like they hadn't been ironed since they'd been bought off the rack. Oglesby noticed Rick and called to him.

"Rick, is that how you keep your svelte figure? I am envious."

Rick walked over. "Don't bother getting up, gentlemen, I'm going up to shower before I catch a chill. You two are up early. Still arguing over those lost Jacopos?"

"That was quite a rousing discussion yesterday, wasn't it?" Muller's English, thanks to study and lectureships at Cambridge, was almost more British than Oglesby's. "I was expecting fisticuffs at one point." He grinned, his mouth matching the shape of his gray mustache.

The Englishman huffed. "The man should be barred from academic discourse."

"Now, now, George," answered Muller. "Fortuna has a right to his opinions."

"It's the way he expresses them, Karl, you know that."

Rick looked down at the two men. "Sorry I brought up the subject, you appeared to be having a pleasant conversation before I arrived."

"Not your fault, Rick," said Oglesby. "We were discussing family history, of all things. It appears that Karl and I have something else in common that connects us with Italy. Both our grandfathers were in the Italian theater during the war."

"Really? You mean they could have—?"

"Been shooting at each other?" the German interjected. "Let's hope not, but I suppose it's possible. If so, I'm pleased they both missed."

Both men were still laughing when Rick excused himself and walked to the elevator.

He stayed in the shower longer than usual. With the conference over he did not have to be at the museum to check the equipment and work out the day's drill with his fellow translator. She had left after that final, lively session of the afternoon, anxious to return to a young daughter who was with her grandmother. Rick, however, had planned for a few days of vacation after the final session, anxious to explore an area of Italy unfamiliar to him. As a kid, when his family had lived in Rome, their vacations had been spent mostly visiting his mother's relatives around Italy, and none lived in the Veneto. They'd gone to Venice, of course, and some of the larger cities in the region, but not smaller towns like Bassano. Most of his translation work took place in the major cities of Italy, so the occasional job off the tourist track made a welcome change and a chance to explore. Why move from New Mexico to Italy otherwise?

After shaving, he slipped on some casual slacks and pulled on a pair of comfortably worn cowboy boots. The *lucida scarpe* towelette he'd found among the soap and shampoo in the basket next to the sink had barely made a difference on them, but it was better than nothing. Perhaps if he ran into the cleaning girl in the hallway he'd ask her to leave him a few extras. He slipped a sweater over his sports shirt, brushed his hair into place, and headed for the door. One thing about doing an early run, it made breakfast taste even better.

He stopped at the doorway of the hotel dining room and surveyed the tables. Most were filled with Austrian tourists, given their dress and the proximity of that country to Bassano. A group of the students from the seminar sat at a large table, looking like they had been up most of the night. They huddled silently over their coffee cups. Two men he recognized from the seminar were at a table on the far side of the room. Franco Sarchetti, who was staying at the hotel, sat before a large plate of food. Rick once again wondered about the man's reason for attending the program. He was an art dealer from Milan, rather than a scholar of Jacopo Bassano, but he had paid his fee and sat through all of the sessions, occasionally making informed comments during the question periods. His breakfast companion was Paolo Tibaldi, the curator of the museum that had hosted the program. Rick assumed Tibaldi had come by the hotel to say goodbye to any participants still there, but it was interesting that he was sitting with Sarchetti.

Rather than join them, Rick walked toward a table where a gray-haired man sat alone, bent over a coffee cup and a book. Taddeo Gaddi, the oldest of the seminar panelists, wore his usual rumpled suit and squinted through thick glasses at the pages.

"Do you mind if I join you, Dottore?"

The man looked up and focused on Rick's face. "Ah, Riccardo, *buon giorno*. Of course. I thought you had left already. You live in Rome, don't you?" He reached into the book and pulled out a thin piece of paper to mark his place while Rick took a seat.

"Yes, but I'm going to take a few days off to see more of this part of the Veneto." An apron-clad girl arrived at the table and Rick asked for *caffè latte*. As she turned to leave he stopped her and ordered scrambled eggs with bacon and toast. She noted his room number from the key he'd placed on the table, nodded, and walked toward the kitchen. Rick answered the look on Gaddi's face. "I usually just go to the buffet, but while I was doing my morning run today I couldn't get eggs and bacon out of my head."

"I would expect nothing less from an American."

"My mother is a Romana, so I am also Italian."

Gaddi smiled. "I've never seen an Italian wearing boots like yours, Riccardo."

He decided against his usual comment on how comfortable they were. "I hope you enjoyed the seminar. I found it fascinating, but of course I knew little about Jacopo Bassano before arriving."

"Jacopo," the old man said simply before taking a sip from his coffee cup. "He is not well known unless you are from this town, or study the period as the distinguished panelists at this seminar do." Rick noticed Gaddi's emphasis on the word *distinguished*. "Like any specialty, it can be arcane for the average person, even an educated person. But that is what we academics do. Most people have the idea that professors are there to make a subject understandable to their students, but they could not be more mistaken. A successful academic must make his specialty as abstruse and incomprehensible as possible, so that his expertise generates awe and sells textbooks. And he gets invited to seminars. But perhaps I have become too cynical in my later years. You have spent some time at the university, Riccardo?"

"A *laurea* and masters in languages, in America."

"Of course, that would make sense for your profession."

Rick's eggs and bacon arrived, their aroma reminding him how hungry he was. The professor wished him a *buon appetito* and topped off his own coffee cup from the pitcher on the table.

"I was fascinated," said Rick between bites, "by the exchange yesterday between Tibaldi and Professor Fortuna about those two missing Jacopo Bassano paintings. It got quite heated."

Gaddi, a frown spreading over his face, watched Rick butter his toast. After a deep breath he spoke. "The subject appears to be a painful one for our host, since he wants his museum to be the principal repository of Jacopo's work. But of course Fortuna knew that and used it to make the poor man uncomfortable. Despite that, I found it surprising that Tibaldi lashed out, albeit briefly."

"My guess is that Fortuna would not win a popularity contest among the participants." Rick noticed that the topic was clearly making the older man uncomfortable. "You are returning home today, Professor?"

"Not yet, I have some personal matters to deal with in Bassano." He glanced at the table where the Milanese art dealer and the museum curator were still talking. "And there is some research on Jacopo I wanted to do in the museum archives. For a monograph I'm working on. I should be able to do everything today and leave early tomorrow."

"Several other participants have opted to stay on past the seminar. But Muller is driving home this afternoon, I believe, and Oglesby may be flying back to London. Professor Randolph told me at the dinner last night he'll be staying on for a few days."

"Which is understandable," said Gaddi, "coming all the way from America. Randolph mentioned something about his fiancée joining him for a bit of a holiday."

"That must be why he was in such a good mood at the dinner. I thought it was the wine." Rick glanced around the room. "And Fortuna?"

"Perhaps he skulked off under the cover of darkness." He looked at Rick's empty plate. "*Ha mangiato volentieri?*"

"It was just what I needed to face the morning, Professor."

The older man rose from his chair. "If you'll excuse me, Riccardo, I must also face the morning. If I don't see you before you depart, it was a pleasure." He held out his hand.

Rick got to his feet and found that the handshake was firm despite the man's bony fingers. He watched Gaddi walk with short steps out of the dining room, thinking about the man's negative reaction to a mention of the missing paintings. All it had done for Rick was add to his curiosity about them. Possibly the only one of the seminar experts who would talk to him about the lost Jacopos would be Fortuna, and Rick had no desire to ask his opinion. A pompous speech would be all he'd get from the man, and he'd had to translate enough of them during the seminar. He poured himself a fresh mixture of coffee and hot milk and stirred in sugar before glancing at the buffet table. A yoghurt? An orange? Why not? He took his napkin from his lap, placed it next to his empty plate, got to his feet. He stopped. *Of course—why didn't I think of it before? I'll call him after breakfast.*

He strode to the food table thinking that one of those sweet rolls would go well with what remained in his coffee cup.

Rick pushed open the glass door of the hotel with one hand and pulled his cell phone from his pocket with the other. The night's chill was clinging to the air, but the sun was well over the horizon and spreading warmth over the hills and valleys that surrounded Bassano. He scrolled through names on the phone's screen as a dark blue car pulled up and a man in a matching suit emerged from the back and stood at the curb while closing one of the buttons on his jacket. He leaned over, spoke to the driver through the passenger-side window, and turned toward the hotel entrance. After one step he noticed Rick.

"Riccardo, *buon giorno.*" It was as much a statement as a greeting.

Rick put his phone away and extended his hand. "*Buon giorno,* Dottor Porcari."

If Rick and his Uncle Piero had spotted Stefano Porcari when playing their "guess the profession" game, both would have immediately pegged him as a banker. It would have been too easy. Porcari was the vice president of the local bank which sponsored the seminar, sparing no expense, especially on the posters all around town which prominently featured the bank name and logo. Banco di Bassano proudly supported the community, and there was no better way to do it than through culture, especially when it involved Bassano's most famous native son.

"You are returning to Rome today, Riccardo?"

"I'm staying a few extra days to see the sights."

"Excellent. If I can be of any assistance, of course you will let me know."

"Thank you, Dottore. Are you here to see someone from the seminar? Some of them are still here."

Porcari momentarily looked blank, then snapped out of it. "Why, yes."

"I saw Muller and Oglesby earlier in the lobby, and Gaddi and Sarchetti were in the dining room. I doubt if they have checked out yet."

"*Grazie*, Riccardo, I'll track them down." He looked at his watch and Rick wondered if he had a set appointment with someone. But he was the kind of person who checked his watch frequently. Must be a banker thing.

Rick again pulled his phone from his pocket once Porcari had disappeared into the building. He found the number he was searching for and tapped it. After five rings he was about to hang up when a familiar voice came on the line.

"Rick, I thought you were in Bassano del Grappa confusing people with your translations."

Beppo Rinaldi, Rick's high school buddy, had surprised everyone when he got a position with the art police when he left the university. He'd been voted most likely to succeed by his classmates at the American School of Rome, but they assumed his success would be in industry. Indeed, they would have been surprised if he were not successful, since his father owned the company. But instead of studying business he chose art history, and now, instead of worrying about the bottom line, he concerned himself with finding stolen art. Rick was still amazed.

"I am indeed in Bassano, *caro* Beppo, and the seminar in which I plied my trade has ended. Something came up during it, however, which has piqued my curiosity, and you are the man who can provide edification."

"I am always ready to edify *un vecchio amico*, Rick. What is your question?"

Rick told him that the seminar theme was Jacopo Bassano, and one of the topics that had surfaced, with some short but heated discussion, was about two lost paintings by the master.

"I know Jacopo, of course, and I vaguely remember hearing about those two paintings when I started working here. I suspect they are in our cold case files, since we have enough recent thefts to keep us busy. But I recall that in Bassano…let me check something." Rick could hear the sound of keyboard strokes. "Yes, here it is. Rick, I know I can trust you to keep this confidential, but we do have a man up there who has helped us over the years with some of our cases. Pro bono, of course. I've never had the need to contact the man, but he is highly regarded. Can you write this down?"

Rick, ever the professional translator, always carried a pen and note pad to jot down new words. He pressed the phone against his ear and pulled them out. "I'm flattered that you would entrust such information to me, Beppo. OK, I'm ready."

"I trust you more than many of my colleagues, Rick. This place can be a den of vipers. The man's name is Fabio Innocenti, and he runs an art gallery on Piazza Monte Vecchio."

"I think I noticed the gallery on my morning run today."

"You have to stop this exercising, Rick. You're going to give yourself a heart attack." There was a pause, and Rick could hear Beppo typing on his computer. "Hmm. This is interesting. It appears that these Jacopo da Bassano paintings are not in the cold case files. There have been some rumblings coming out of Milan."

"Rumblings? What does that mean?"

More typing. "Not sure. When you see Innocenti, tell him you were given his name by Captain Scuderi. No need to mention my name."

No need? Rick knew his buddy well enough to understand that Beppo's name should be kept well out of it. He assumed Captain Scuderi was lower on the office organizational chart, but he was never sure how the art cops worked, despite an earlier collaboration with the ministry. "Scuderi is Innocenti's handler?"

"You've been reading too many spy novels, Rick, and we don't use that term here."

"Sorry." He slipped the note pad back in his pocket. "When I get back to Rome I'll tell you if I found anything of interest from Signor Innocenti and you can pass it to Captain Scuderi."

Beppo was typing again. "That will be most appreciated."

"My guess, from the exchanges I heard at the conference, is that the two paintings will never be found."

"Which increases the value of the ones that are known, keeps them rare."

"I never thought of that, Beppo."

"The art community is a jungle, Rick. So when are you back in the Eternal City?"

"In a few days, unless I get bored."

"I'm sure you'll find some excitement." The desk phone rang. "Have to go. Let me know if anything turns up."

Rick slipped his cell phone in his jacket pocket. The conversation confirmed his sense that something was going on with the two paintings. This would be more fun than simultaneous interpretation.

Chapter Three

Three police cars drew up in front of the hotel, lights flashing. From the first, three uniformed policemen jumped out, while a man in civilian dress emerged slowly from the back of the second car. Inspector Giuliano Occasio looked up and down the street before walking to the door of the hotel, already being held open by one of his men. Of the policemen in the assemblage, he was the shortest, and the only one sporting facial hair, a pencil-thin mustache. Followed by three of the uniformed police and another plain clothes officer, he strode directly to the reception desk where a clerk watched them approach.

"I am Inspector Occasio. Get the manager." After speaking the words, he studied his fingernails and looked around the lobby. Two foreign tourists who had been making decisions on what to see that morning looked up from their guide books to watch the show. The clerk, who had rushed through a door behind the desk, reappeared with an older man who also wore the hotel logo on the pocket of his blazer.

"May I be of assistance, Inspector?"

"I am looking for Signor Tibaldi. They told me at the museum that he was here."

"Dottor Tibaldi, of the museum? He's been over here various times in the last few days in connection with the museum's seminar, since all the official participants were staying at the hotel, but I—"

"Excuse me sir," the clerk interrupted, "but I think I saw him going into the dining room earlier."

"Get him," said the policeman, while keeping his eyes on the manager. The clerk scuttled around the counter and walked quickly across the lobby into the dining room, followed by the eyes of the two tourists. "Do you have a list of the seminar participants who are at the hotel? I'll need to see it." The manager shuffled through some papers below the counter and came up with two typewritten sheets stapled together. He passed them to the policeman who glanced at them and passed them back. "I'd like ten copies. And if these people are in the hotel at this moment, I want them called and told to come to the lobby."

The manager finally regained his voice. "Inspector, can I ask what—?"

"You'll be told in due time." He turned around to see Tibaldi coming into the lobby, followed by the desk clerk. "Don't forget those calls," he said, his order meant for the manager behind him.

"What seems to be the trouble, Inspector?" Paolo Tibaldi frowned when he reached the policeman.

"Let's talk over there, Signor Tibaldi." He gestured toward a corner of the lobby arranged with chairs and a sofa set up for conversation. The clerk rushed to Occasio and handed him the copies. The policeman took them without a word of thanks. The two men sat down across from each other, two of the uniformed policeman standing nearby to assure privacy. Occasio looked at Tibaldi and leaned back in the chair. "Professor Lorenzo Fortuna."

"Yes, Inspector, he is one of the distinguished participants in the seminar that ended yesterday. You've likely noticed our posters around town. But I haven't seen him yet this morning."

"And you won't. He's been found dead." He paused to observe Tibaldi's reaction.

"I, I can't believe that," was the stuttered reply. "He seemed in good health, though perhaps a bit overweight. He did enjoy his wine. Some kind of heart attack?"

Occasio ignored the question. "According to the program found in his pocket, you were the organizer of the seminar."

"Well, yes, Inspector. I suppose I should take charge of notifying his family and seeing that his body is—"

"That won't be necessary." Occasio's expression changed little as he spoke, nor did his flat monotone. "I should make myself clear. Fortuna did not die of natural causes, he was murdered. Which is why I am here. I or one of my men will be interviewing you and all of the participants in the seminar. The program said that the final event was a dinner last evening, is that correct?"

The question managed to penetrate Tibaldi's dazed state. "Yes, the dinner. It was held at a restaurant a few blocks from here. Fortuna was there, along with all the other distinguished invitees, as well as the director of the museum and the managers of the Banco di Bassano, which sponsored the seminar."

"What time did the dinner end?"

Tibaldi looked up to see an annoyed Franco Sarchetti talking with a man in a dark suit whom he guessed to be another policeman. Between the art dealer and the policeman, the banker stood silently, a blank look on his face. Behind them Oglesby and Muller, watched by a uniformed policeman, huddled together and stared at Inspector Occasio.

"It must have been around nine thirty, perhaps close to ten, when the dinner ended. There were toasts, some remarks by Dottor Porcari." He gestured toward the banker.

"Porcari is here?" The inspector turned and looked. "Excellent. Who is that man with him, other than my detective?"

"That is Signor Sarchetti, another participant in the seminar."

Occasio consulted his list. "Milanese, owns an art gallery." Tibaldi nodded, but the policeman didn't notice. "Who from the group at the dinner is not in the lobby now?"

Tibaldi rubbed his chin in thought. "Well, Professor Gaddi— there he is now, that older gentleman. I don't see Professor Randolph, the American. The director of the museum, of course, my superior; he is at his office. I think that's it. Oh, our interpreter, Riccardo Montoya; he will not be listed on the program. Our other interpreter departed after the final seminar session."

The policeman frowned. "You mean everyone does not speak Italian?"

"No, Inspector, many do not. The conference was conducted in Italian and English, with simultaneous interpretation."

Occasio shook his head in disgust. "I will need this Montoya."

Rick entered the elevator hoping he didn't look too much like a tourist. No camera hung from around his neck, but he did have a red-covered *Touring Club Italiano* guide to the Veneto region in one hand. To the average resident of Bassano the book would brand him as an Italian tourist, though the cowboy boots would certainly confuse them. When he stepped into the lobby, his concerns about appearance vanished.

Uniformed policemen were everywhere, and he quickly spotted two men who had the look of police detectives. Three of the experts from the seminar—Muller, Oglesby, and Gaddi—sat silently along the wall of the room, a policeman beside them. Franco Sarchetti occupied a chair by himself near the door, talking with the man whom Rick assumed was also a policeman. Paolo Tibaldi of the museum stood near a window, his head bent in thought. Sitting with one of the two detectives was Porcari, the banker he'd greeted on the street. The policeman maintained an ingratiating smile on his face as he talked to the banker. Rick walked toward them and was stopped by the uplifted arm of another policeman.

"Please stay where you are, sir. Are you a guest at the hotel?"

"Yes. What's going on?"

"Were you involved with the art program? The seminar?"

"Yes, I was. Does this have anything to do with the seminar?"

The cop again ignored Rick's question as he got the attention of the plainclothes officer talking with Sarchetti. He excused himself to the art dealer and walked quickly to Rick. Unlike the one with the thin mustache sitting with the banker, this policeman appeared to possess a genuine smile.

"This man just came out of the elevator, sir. He says he was part of the museum program."

"I'm Riccardo Montoya." He offered his hand and the policeman shook it.

"Detective Alfredo DiMaio. I don't recall seeing your name on the list of participants, Signor Montoya."

"I was one of two interpreters who did the simultaneous translation. I'm not one of the art experts."

The detective nodded his head toward the three sitting nearby. "After translating for these people for a few days you must have become an expert by osmosis. At any rate, we'll have to question you, too, so if you could take a seat—"

"Detective, you haven't told me what's going on."

The man held up his hands in mock defense. "So I have not. It seems that someone in your group has gotten himself murdered. A certain Professor Fortuna."

"Fortuna, murdered?" Rick's eyes darted around the room.

"The body isn't here."

Rick's face snapped back but he saw immediately that DiMaio wore a benign smile.

"Yes, of course, Detective. When did it happen?"

"The way this works, Signor Montoya, is that we ask the questions."

"Naturally. How can I be of help?"

"Thank you for asking. Inspector Occasio will decide if he or I will question you. In the meantime, please have a seat. You can read your guidebook while you wait." He walked to the inspector, who was still talking with Porcari, and leaned over to say something in his superior's ear. Occasio looked back at Rick quickly, the frown returning to his face. He answered his detective with a wave of the hand and returned to his conversation with the banker.

There was a seat next to Professor Gaddi and Rick took it. Gaddi's face had always shown its years, but since their conversation at breakfast it seemed to have added a few shadows. He stared blankly at Rick as if he just now recognized him. "Can you believe this, Riccardo?"

"A very nasty business, Professor."

"Nasty, indeed. We had enough excitement during the seminar, most of it due to Fortuna, but we didn't need this to cap things off. A murder. Who would have imagined it?"

"Must have been a robbery gone wrong. Who would want to murder the man?"

Gaddi's face formed into a twisted smile. "Who?" He waved his hands at the others. "The line forms over there. I don't think there's anyone in our seminar, except for you, who did not feel the sting of Fortuna's tongue, or the viciousness of his pen at some time or another. And the man took great pleasure in it all. To say that he will not be missed among most of the art history community would be an understatement."

The detective returned and Rick rose to his feet. "Inspector Occasio would like me to interview you first, but then he needs you to translate when he talks to the people who don't speak Italian." DiMaio smiled; apparently he found this humorous. "Let's go into the dining room. There could be some food left over from breakfast, you never know."

The staff had cleared all the tables and was setting up for lunch. The two men took seats at a table at the far end of the room.

"Why don't I begin with the classic question?" said the policeman as he pulled out his note pad.

"That would be 'Where were you, Signor Montoya, between the hours of nine o'clock and—let me guess—four a.m.'"

"*Bravo*. I could not be more impressed." He pulled a pen from his jacket and waited.

"I left the dinner at about nine-thirty. I think I was one of the first to head back to the hotel. By that time everyone had gotten up from their seats and they were sipping grappa. I am not a big fan of the drink, so I thanked the bank president, our host, and slipped out. I like to check my mail in the evening to see what has come in from friends in America, because of the time zones."

"You lived in America, Signor Montoya? That's where you got your boots, I suppose."

"My father is American, so I have both citizenships."

"I have a cousin who lives in America, perhaps you know him. He lives in someplace called Staten Island." He looked at Rick's face and laughed. "I am making the *piccolo scherzo*, of course."

"You'd be surprised how many people have asked me that and been serious, Detective."

"Not all Italians are as sharp as we policemen are. Anyway, no one left the restaurant with you?"

"No, I walked back alone."

"Was Fortuna still there when you departed? Did you happen to see who he was with?"

"He was still there, of that I'm sure. Everyone was standing around in small groups, I can't recall who was speaking with whom."

DiMaio nodded and drew tiny squares on his pad. "During the conference, did you notice anything unusual between Fortuna and any of the other participants? You were at all the sessions, I assume."

"I was. Well, I suppose you know about the time when Fortuna and Professor Gaddi started punching each other."

DiMaio's head jerked up, but when he saw Rick's expression, a wide grin opened across his face. "Ah, it was your turn for the *piccolo scherzo*. Let me mark that down in the book: DiMaio one, Montoya one."

"Forgive me, Detective, I couldn't resist." Rick was starting to like DiMaio. "But to be serious—"

"No need to be serious, we're only conducting a murder investigation here."

"Of course. As I was about to say, Fortuna would not have been characterized as warm and congenial, if I may understate. During the seminar he frequently found fault in the presentations of the other participants, and enjoyed pointing them out in the most acerbic manner possible. Such behavior does not go over well in the academic community, as you may imagine, where everyone is usually polite even if they think the other person's scholarship might be lacking. I saw it happen several times during the program. On the final day, for example, there was an exchange about two missing paintings that elicited some strong reactions from Fortuna. And it was not always easy to translate the man's comments, given the venom that was often inserted in them."

DiMaio had been writing as Rick talked. "Were there any of these exchanges, if that's the word, which were especially…"

"Violent? Enough to make the person want to do Fortuna in? I don't recall any one that stood out. And Fortuna treated everyone the same. Of course I witnessed only what took place this week."

The policeman looked up from his notes. "Of course. An old academic wound caused by Fortuna could have been festering, if I might make a medical analogy, and last night the opportunity to exact revenge presented itself."

"But I can't picture any of these scholars exacting revenge for anything," Rick said as he caught the eyes of one of the waitresses clearing the tables and preparing them for lunch. She quickly averted her glance and went back to work. "Not that academics are incapable of violence, but this group…I just don't see it."

The detective tapped his pen on the table and then closed his pad. "Let me ask you something else, Signor Montoya, which is not related to the investigation." His face grinned as his eyes bored in on Rick. "I can tell from your face you are intrigued. You're thinking, this cop is trying to catch me off guard in order to trick me into saying something I didn't intend. Then, next thing you know, I'm peering out at him from behind bars, asking for a lawyer. Then—"

"Detective, what's your question?"

The smile turned to disappointment. "Well, Signor Montoya, at the police academy I had an instructor who I recall told us he had an American nephew. Furthermore, this nephew worked as—"

"Commissario Fontana is my uncle, Detective."

The policeman slipped the leather notebook into his pocket while keeping his eyes on Rick. "*Pensa un po'*, the nephew of Commissario Fontana, right here. This should make things more interesting." The pen was inserted in the same pocket. "You never thought of following your uncle into police work? You could get on the bullhorn and yell 'We've got you surrounded, come out with your hands up' in two languages."

"That would be helpful. But let me ask you a question, even though you're the one who's supposed to handle that part of the interrogation, Detective. Do you usually encourage suspects in murder investigations to join the police force?"

DiMaio rose to his feet. "I suppose that, strictly speaking, you are a suspect, despite your family connection with Commissario Fontana. So I'll wait until the murderer is apprehended before asking you again about any future plans to change professions."

They walked back into the lobby. Inspector Occasio was now leaning forward in his seat, pointing a finger at a terrified Professor Gaddi who pressed himself back into the chair opposite the policeman.

"I know I'm only supposed to be asking questions, Signor Montoya, but let me offer one piece of advice," said DiMaio as they watched the scene. "You may not want to mention to the inspector that you're the nephew of Commissario Fontana."

Occasio, through an underling, assigned Rick a time to be at the hotel to help with the questioning of the non-Italian speakers. It didn't give him enough time to see any sights, but Rick had time to look in on Signor Innocenti, the art cops' man in Bassano. As he walked the few blocks to the Piazza Monte Vecchio he pondered the new development. Could any of the seminar participants be behind the murder of Fortuna? To begin with, it didn't seem in character for any of them. The only speaker who had forcefully confronted one of the man's snide comments was the museum curator, Tibaldi, but it was a minor dustup by any standard, and, after it, the seminar deliberations had returned to the usual scholarly jargon. Had it been a bar on Central Avenue, one of the men might have demanded to settle things in the parking lot, but this wasn't Albuquerque. No, the motive had to be something that predated the seminar.

What was it that Uncle Piero always told him? Money, passion, or honor; one of the three was sure to be involved if someone is murdered. Passion from a wronged husband? That didn't seem likely with Fortuna. Honor? Perhaps. Money? The most probable.

The sidewalks on the square were protected by the extended second floors of the buildings, supported at the curb side by rounded columns. Window shopping and strolling under the porticoes was a popular activity in the north of Italy, where rain was a normal part of every late fall and spring. And in the heat of summer, the sidewalks were equally attractive thanks to their cool shade. The connected sidewalks made it possible to make the rounds of shops in total protection before moving to another square.

Rick immediately spotted Arte Innocenti, a shop positioned between a pharmacy and a shirt store, as he entered the square. Its large window was sparsely decorated; two paintings on wooden easels between a low curtain and the glass. Behind them he could see that other works similar to the two—brightly colored abstracts—hung from the walls. Likely a one-man show, perhaps a local artist. He stood at the glass and studied the two on display, but quickly noticed a young woman working at a small laptop at a lone desk in the corner of the room. Her short black hair was accented by a pair of dangly earrings whose colors matched those of the paintings behind her. Her features were soft, she wore dark half glasses, and Rick estimated her age to be around thirty. When she took her left hand from the keyboard and brushed back her hair, he noted that she wore no rings. As he was thinking of the significance of ring-less fingers, she looked up, noticed him, and smiled. It was not an unpleasant smile. He stepped to the door and went in.

"*Buon giorno.*" Her voice went with the smile.

"*Buon giorno.* I was looking for Signor Innocenti. Is he here?"

She rose to her feet and Rick noticed her figure. "He's in the back. May I have your name?"

"Montoya, Riccardo Montoya. But he is not expecting me. Please tell him that I was recommended to him by Captain Scuderi."

The smile remained, but visibly tightened. So much for Beppo's secret operations, Rick thought. The woman knows. And if she worked with Innocenti on stolen art, why hadn't Beppo given me her name instead?

She excused herself and went through a door behind the desk. Rick walked to one of the paintings, a mass of color, and tried to decipher if there was something represented in the swirls and lines. He concluded that it was purely abstract, and also that it was not something he would hang in his apartment, not that there was much room on its walls anyway. He also saw a small, red dot stuck to the bottom of the glass, meaning that someone liked it enough to buy it. No price displayed, of course. That would be in a book on the table. As he was trying to guess how many euros it had set the buyer back, a man appeared from the back room, followed by the girl. He wore a brown suit with a pale yellow shirt and print tie. His thin gray hair started about a third of the way over his head, getting thicker as it reached the back of his neck, giving him the look of an orchestra conductor. As he reached out his hand, Rick thought he looked vaguely familiar.

"Fabio Innocenti, Signor Montoya, *un piacere.*"

"*Piacere mio*, Signor Innocenti. Have we met before?"

The man's smile remained, but a questioning look was added to it. "I don't believe so. Is this your first visit to Bassano?" The girl's eyes moved back to Rick.

"It is, but I've been here for several days, at a seminar—of course, that's where I've seen you, at the Jacopo seminar."

"Yes, I attended some of the sessions. I was sitting in the back with the students and other interested public. I don't remember seeing you, however."

"You wouldn't have if you were watching the speakers. I was in the translation booth behind you, wearing earphones and talking into a microphone."

"Ah, but now I recognize your voice." He turned to the girl. "Isn't that interesting, Elizabetta, that I would know his voice but not his face?"

"Like listening to the radio, *Babbo.*"

"You met my daughter, Signor Montoya?"

"I have now." He was close enough, when he took her hand, also to take in her perfume. As he always did, Rick tried to identify the perfume, but was too distracted by the face to come up with a name. The reading glasses had been removed and he noticed that her eyes were a deep green and large. Very large.

"But please sit down, Signor Montoya." He gestured toward a group of chairs at one end of the open room. "Captain Scuderi just called to alert me that you would be dropping in. Something about old works of art?"

Rick took a seat across from the man and his daughter. "My contact in the ministry is an old friend. In truth, I have not met the captain."

Innocenti grinned. "We've never met either. In person, that is, only spoken on the phone."

Lots of practice in recognizing voices, Rick thought before speaking. "My reason for calling on you is not official, but my friend thought you could help me with some questions I have about an issue that came up at the seminar."

"I would be pleased to help if I can. I was asked to extend every courtesy. That sounds very formal, but I trust it means that in the ministry you are held in high regard. Now tell me, what is the issue?"

"The missing Jacopos."

Innocenti raised his hands and his eyes toward the ceiling before looking again at Rick. "What can I say? You heard about them at the seminar."

"Which is why I became curious. Were you at that last session when Professor Fortuna and Signor Tibaldi of the museum got into it about the two paintings?"

"I was. It was good to see someone returning fire at Fortuna. Did I tell you about the man, *Cara*?"

"The nasty one, *Babbo*?"

"Nasty isn't strong enough to describe him. Though he does know his art history, especially that regarding Jacopo da Bassano."

Rick made a quick calculation and decided that news of Fortuna's murder would reach the whole town quickly. No need to keep silent about it. "Signor Innocenti, Fortuna was found dead this morning. The police are at the hotel now interviewing the seminar participants."

"*Dio mio,*" Innocenti gasped and exchanged glances with his daughter. "Police? They don't expect foul play, do they?"

"It appears they do. But tell me about the two lost Jacopos. Not that they would have anything to do with Fortuna's death."

"I certainly hope not." He rubbed his chin and again looked over at his daughter. She nodded quickly. "But I have to tell you, Signor Montoya, the reason I attended the seminar is that I have a hunch something is happening regarding those missing paintings."

"Really? From listening to the few comments about them, I got the impression that they will never be found."

"That may be true. As I said, it is a hunch. I have not even told Captain Scuderi about it, since I don't have anything concrete. Why get the art police involved if my instincts turn out to be unfounded?"

Rick was puzzled. Beppo had let slip that there was some movement in the art police on this case, but apparently Scuderi hadn't passed that news to Innocenti during their phone call. Or Scuderi had said something and Innocenti didn't want to tell Rick. Did Beppo trust Rick more than Scuderi trusted Innocenti? This would take some sorting out.

"Do you know the history of these two paintings, Signor Montoya?"

"No, that's why I called my friend in Rome. And he gave me your name."

Innocenti sat back in his chair and rubbed his hands together in thought. "The two paintings were from the period in his career when Jacopo was influenced more by Venetian masters, though, as you know from the seminar, he always lived here in Bassano. They were owned by a wealthy Venetian family which had them hung in their vacation villa just outside Bassano, near Asolo.

During the war, anyone with art of value had hidden it away to keep it from the Nazis, but the family apparently thought that they were isolated enough that no one would notice.

"In those last days of the war this part of Italy was in total chaos. Allied troops were working their way north, held back by retreating Germans as they went. And the Italian partisans were hiding in the hills, coming down only to ambush Germans or make their departure difficult before disappearing again. It was anarchy. During that time the paintings went missing. The family had fled to the liberated regions to the south, and when they returned here after the Veneto had come under Allied control, they found their villa ransacked and the paintings gone. At the time it was assumed that a German column had passed the house on its way to Austria and stolen the paintings, but it has never been proven. The Nazis kept good records, but not of that sort of activity. It is possible, of course, that they were taken by one of the liberating armies, or even some Italians who knew they were there, but I doubt it. The German theory, given their history of plundering art, seems the most likely."

Rick immediately thought of Muller's grandfather, but said nothing. It was Elizabetta Innocenti who spoke next. "My father has always been interested in these paintings, as you would expect of someone born in Bassano. I am not so sure that it was the Germans, Riccardo. Do you mind if I call you Riccardo?"

"Please do."

"And everyone except my father calls me Betta."

Rick was concentrating on Betta when he realized the time. "I'm afraid I have to get back to the hotel. The police inspector wants me to translate when he talks with the foreign participants." He got to his feet, followed by the two Innocentis. "I'd like to learn more about the two paintings. And if there is some way, Signor Innocenti, that I could help with your…"

With some difficulty due to the tightness of her slacks, Betta pulled a card from her pocket. "Here is the phone number of the gallery, and my cell. My father doesn't believe in cell phones."

As he crossed the piazza, Rick could not get Betta out of his mind, but when he got closer to the hotel he remembered he was about to have his first encounter with Inspector Occasio.

Chapter Four

The hotel lobby was calmer now; only a few uniformed police stood in one corner, trying to look busy or at least somewhat official. Rick spotted Detective DiMaio seated in one of the lush lobby chairs, talking on his cell phone. From the smile on the man's face Rick assumed it was a personal call, but perhaps he was naturally cheerful. The first impression was certainly a positive one, unlike that made by DiMaio's boss, even though Rick had yet to be introduced to Inspector Occasio. DiMaio waved Rick over before saying a few words into his phone and slipping it into his pocket.

"Sit down, Riccardo. Do you mind if I call you Riccardo?"

"Not at all." Everyone, it seemed, wanted to call him by his first name. Would Inspector Occasio do the same? He thought not.

"And I am Alfredo, please, except in front of the inspector. Could upset the man." DiMaio settled back in the chair, its red velvet matching the burgundy of his tie. "He should be ready for you to translate in a moment. He's talking with the prosecuting attorney now about the case."

Rick looked at the detective and pondered what he had just heard. Was this a variation on the good cop, bad cop routine? It was going on a year now that Rick had been living in Italy, and he had worried that he was adopting the cynicism for which the Romans are known. Never take anything at face value—always assume there is something behind every comment—look for a motive in the most innocuous of actions. In Rick's head it was happening now. DiMaio seemed like a decent fellow, but was he real? A phone call to his uncle would help answer the question, but he wasn't sure if he wanted to do that. At least not yet.

"How did the interviews with the Italians go? If you don't mind me asking."

DiMaio glanced at a door at the far end of the lobby. Rick assumed Inspector Occasio was secreted behind it, and that the detective was deciding how to answer. It took a few moments to get the reply.

"Why should I mind? One thing for sure, there was universal agreement that Professor Fortuna will not be missed, as you mentioned this morning. The guy must have been a real *stronzo*, if you'll pardon the expression. Alas, none of the men has a strong alibi for the time that our victim likely met his end." A thin smile appeared on his face. "As is the case with you, Riccardo.

Rick let the comment pass, and the policeman continued.

"I did not sit in on the questioning of Dottor Porcari. My superior felt that for a man of such stature in the community— the vice president of Bassano's leading bank, after all—that for such a personage he, the inspector, should deal with the man personally. So I took the opportunity to have a coffee next door. I know the owner."

"But the others? There must have been something of interest besides establishing alibis." Rick wondered if he was pushing too hard.

DiMaio frowned in thought. "Tibaldi, the man from the museum, he was the most nervous of the lot. Hands were actually shaking, you should have seen it. He kept saying how terrible it was for the museum, that the event had been such a success and now this murder would overshadow it. On and on. His concern is understandable, of course. He organizes this international event but now the newspapers will only write that one of his art experts croaked. But Tibaldi, too, had no alibi. He said he went back to the museum to take care of things after the close of the seminar."

"Folding and stacking the chairs in the conference room."

"What?" He pointed at Rick. "I like that. Folding chairs. That's good." He glanced around the room and lowered his voice. "But let me tell you, Riccardo, the one person who is most troubling to me is Sarchetti, the Milanese guy who sells art. I'm not sure if my *capo* got the same feeling about the man, though. Occasio's not one to share his theories with me or anyone else."

"Will you be part of the interrogation of the three foreigners?"

"There are three? Ah, that's right, the American. He seems to have disappeared for the moment, but we were told he went to the airport to pick up his fiancée. His luggage is still in his room. If he did in Fortuna, he may have decided that a fast getaway is more important than retrieving his clothes. That would be a scene, wouldn't it?—the lady getting off one plane as he's boarding another. Perhaps they wave across the terminal, she with tears in her eyes, not understanding. Could make a good scene in a movie."

"I doubt that Jeffrey Randolph is your murderer, Alfredo."

"You never know, he—"

"DiMaio!"

The voice, somewhat high-pitched, came from the now-open door at the end of the room. A scowling Inspector Occasio caught DiMaio's eye, turned quickly, and disappeared back into the room.

"It looks like we're on next. I'll go get Muller. He and Oglesby are waiting in the bar. If you see Randolph, grab him. Don't let him disappear again." He walked through the lobby to the door into the bar. Rick got to his feet and decided to meet Occasio on his own.

The hotel manager had reluctantly given Occasio the use of a small conference room that looked out on a side street. Any group that needed to meet did not require a mountain view. A large white board hung unused on wall, and a low credenza on one side of the room held a tray with a water carafe and glasses. At the far end of the room's long table the inspector sat, his eyes on a sheaf of papers before him. Despite the click of Rick's heels on the cement floor, the man didn't look up until Rick was at his side.

"I am Riccardo Montoya, Inspector."

Rick's look was met by a pair of squinting eyes. "Yes, I know who you are. Where is DiMaio?" He remained seated and no handshake was offered.

"He went to get Professor Muller."

At that moment DiMaio and Muller appeared at the doorway, introductions were made and the three men took seats at the table. Rick sat next to Muller and DiMaio sat across from them.

"Rick," the German began, "please tell the inspector that I regret my Italian is not—"

"*Zitto*," Occasio snapped, and turned to Rick. "Tell him that I am the person who is conducting the interview."

This is going to be fun.

The questioning of George Oglesby, the art professor, went more smoothly than the interview with the Bavarian Muller because Oglesby exhibited English reserve rather than Teutonic rigidity. But the results were so similar that the two interviews could have been with the same man. The previous evening each had left the dinner alone, returned to his respective hotel room, and turned in. Both had known Fortuna before the seminar, meeting him at other academic conferences. Both were guarded in their opinions of the dead man, but it was clear that neither had been his close friend. Both men, as the interview ended, asked when they would be allowed to leave Bassano, and both were told, in Occasio's brusque manner, to plan on staying put. Rick thought that the policeman could have saved time by simply interviewing one of the two and making a copy of the notes. When Oglesby had left the room Rick got to his feet and started for the door.

"Just a minute, Montoya, there is one more."

DiMaio was still seated next to the inspector. "Sir, Professor Randolph hasn't yet returned from the airport. He went to pick up his—"

"Of course, of course." Occasio waved a hand in front of his face like he was clearing smoke from the room. "If he shows up in the next few minutes, bring him in immediately. Otherwise he'll have to come to the station." He pulled his cell phone from his pocket and dialed a number as if he were the only person in the room. Rick and DiMaio got the hint and left.

Rick closed the conference room door behind him and exchanged smiles with Detective DiMaio. "Did that go as expected, Alfredo?"

"Nobody was injured, was he? So it went well. Your translation was excellent, in spite of the interruptions by Inspector Occasio. I kept picturing you with that bullhorn outside the surrounded hideout. But we didn't get a great deal of new material, to say the least. Those two only confirmed what we already knew from talking to the others. I was hoping that one of them had seen something, either during or after the dinner, that offered some clue. Such as Fortuna arguing with someone outside on the street and challenging him to a duel. Maybe someone lunging at him with a broken bottle. I would have taken something as simple as his leaving the restaurant with someone. No such luck."

"He must have left with someone, or at least arranged to meet someone later. It could have been a person not involved in the seminar, but that seems unlikely. Did he have any friends here in Bassano, or relatives?"

"We're still checking now, but it appears not. You met the guy, do you think he had any friends anywhere? The students who were kissing his *culo* to get good grades don't count."

Rick smiled and nodded. He looked up to see a tall man standing at the reception desk holding what appeared to be a map of the city and peering at it while listening to the desk clerk. His jacket had a herringbone pattern, the shirt under it a tattersall print, and the slacks were a dark brown corduroy. With the clothes, and the touch of gray salted through the blond hair of his temples, he could have stepped off the pages of the Orvis catalog. "You won't have to drag Professor Randolph down to the station, Alfredo. There he is now."

DiMaio eyed the man at the desk. "He looks like an American college professor. What was that movie I saw? Took place in America at some university. I can remember everything about every movie I've seen except the titles. Drives me *pazzo*. If you could bring him into the conference room, I'll tell—"

"Give me a couple minutes with him to explain what's going on. I doubt if he knows."

"If he does know, he's our murderer. We can take him right to the station."

Rick walked to the reception desk. "Professor Randolph, good morning."

He looked up. "Oh, Rick. Good morning. Please, it's Jeff. I was planning out a bit of tourism. Did you know that my fiancée has flown in? She's up in the room getting settled. We're going to see the sights for a few days. Are you also staying on?" This was not the staid voice of the learned professor attending an academic seminar, thought Rick, but that's what love can do. He hated to spoil the mood.

"You may have to put off your tourism, Jeff. Something has come up involving all of us at the seminar." Randolph's expression changed from merriment to bewilderment. "Professor Fortuna has been found dead, and the assumption is foul play. The police have been interviewing everyone who had contact with him the past few days, and they'll need to speak to you. I've been helping the police by translating for the non-Italian participants."

"But…but, that's impossible. Foul play?" His mouth stayed open, twitching, as he searched for words. "It must have been some random act, perhaps a robbery gone wrong. Fortuna was not universally loved, as you must have observed when you were translating, but no one in the seminar could possibly have taken the man's life." Randolph became a professor again, his tone that of an instructor lecturing a class. "I hardly believe that the local police would suspect someone in the academic community of such an act. That would be preposterous."

"They have to consider all possibilities, Jeff. You know how police operate."

"I most certainly do not. I've never even had a speeding ticket."

Rick looked across the lobby to Detective DiMaio, standing at the doorway of the conference room. "The lead policeman, Inspector Occasio, is ready to talk to you, so you should be able to get this over with quickly and start seeing the sights with your fiancée."

Randolph muttered as they crossed the room. Rick introduced him to DiMaio and Occasio, and they took their places at the table. Rick sat between the American and the inspector, so he could translate easily in either direction. He waited while the policeman shuffled through the pages of his notebook. No doubt for dramatic effect.

"You know the drill from translating for the other two, Montoya: whereabouts last night, his previous contacts with Fortuna. Get on with it."

Rick got on with it. Randolph said he had been one of the first to leave, as soon as the formalities had ended, since his fiancée was arriving on an early flight in the morning and he wanted to get a good night's rest. Everyone stood sipping after-dinner drinks when he slipped out and walked back to the hotel. All the participants, including Fortuna, were still there when he left. He didn't notice anyone suspicious standing around outside, not that he would know who would be considered suspicious in an Italian town. He'd never met Fortuna before the seminar, but was very familiar with his work since Randolph could read Italian, even though he had trouble speaking it. Though not asked by Occasio, he expressed his doubts that anyone in the seminar would have reason to murder the man.

As Randolph spoke, and when Rick was translating, Occasio stared at the far wall, not meeting the eyes of either of them. Rick hoped that the professor would not ask him if the policeman was listening, since Occasio would ask for a translation. Fortunately Randolph played it straight, answering the few questions the inspector had as if he were sitting for an oral exam. Translation was easy since he spoke in clear, short sentences. Rick ran out of questions, and neither of the two policemen had anything else to ask. He was about to get to his feet when Occasio, for the first time, trained his eyes on Randolph.

"Montoya, ask the professor where he was between the time the seminar ended yesterday afternoon and the closing dinner in the evening."

As Rick translated, a perplexed look took over Randolph's face.

"In the afternoon? Well, I came back here to change, of course. But…let me see, yes, before that I went down into town. Needed some fresh air after being cooped up in the seminar, and wanted to get a bit of exercise to prepare me for another large meal." He emitted a chortle and cough before again becoming professorial. "They've been feeding us well during our stay in Bassano."

After Rick finished the translation, Occasio continued to stare at Randolph for a few moments before looking at his open notebook. He pulled a pen from his jacket, held it over the paper, and then returned it to the pocket. "Tell him not to leave town."

"What a pleasant man, your Inspector Occasio."

"He's not my inspector, Jeff. But you shouldn't feel singled out for special treatment, he displayed that same pleasant manner with Muller and Oglesby."

Randolph frowned. "And the way he ordered me to stay put. At least he didn't confiscate my passport. It's fortunate that I was planning to stay in Bassano for a few days anyway. I might have been in a pickle if I'd had to return to the university immediately. Thank goodness for graduate assistants."

Rick recalled having to take over a class for much of a semester in grad school when the professor he was working for was interviewing for jobs at other universities. But he kept that story to himself. "Where are you off to today?"

"I think we'll just stay in town, walk around to get a feel for Bassano. Perhaps the ceramics museum. See the covered bridge, of course." His seriousness disappeared as he looked toward the elevator. "There she is, Rick. Come meet Erica."

Rick grabbed a quick breath when he heard the name, and lost his breath completely when he saw the girl walking to the reception desk to drop off the room key. *Of all the hotels in the world, she has to walk into this one.* She wore blue jeans, as would be expected from someone living in the States, but they fit perfectly and had not been purchased at J.C. Penny. Leather boots peeked from below the cuffs. Her hair was longer, its style slightly different, but that one strand still fell loosely over one eye. A light wool jacket over a silk blouse completed the outfit. She was still talking with the reception clerk but he could already smell her perfume, though that may have been his memory in overdrive.

The desk clerk gestured at Professor Randolph and she walked toward him. About halfway across the lobby she noticed Rick and stopped. He had trouble interpreting the look on her face, something between shock and fear, but then she burst out laughing and rushed over.

"Erica, dear, I'd like you to meet—"

"*Ciao,* Ricky." She put her arms around Rick and kissed him on both cheeks.

"It seems that you two have already met."

Rick stayed silent, trying to figure out what to say next. Fortunately Erica spoke first.

"I knew Rick in Rome, Jeffrey."

"At the, uh, university?"

She took Randolph's arm, still looking Rick over in the same way he'd studied her. "No, no. We moved in the same circle of friends. You know how it is."

Rick finally found his tongue. "Your English is fluent, Erica." He immediately cursed himself for such a lame comment.

"*Speriamo bene,* after living all these month in the States." She inclined her head to her fiancé while keeping her eyes on Rick. "Ricky and I always conversed in Italian."

Randolph looked at her with affection. "She's been trying to teach me, but it's rough going, isn't it, Erica?"

She squeezed his arm. "You're doing very well, *caro*. But what are you doing here, Ricky? Were you…of course, you were interpreting at the seminar. What a pleasant coincidence."

It was all too much for Rick to absorb. The last time he'd seen Erica Pedana was over coffee at their favorite bar on Rome's Piazza San Lorenzo in Lucina. It had not been a pleasant encounter, but at that point it hadn't mattered. He was departing the next morning for an interpreter job in Milan, and she was leaving for the States to take a lecturer position in art history. Rick had joked that night that she was taking this decision to move on with their lives too literally, making a transatlantic move. She didn't appreciate the humor, though his jokes had been falling flat for weeks. Her perfume now brought back the memory of their final platonic hug on the piazza before she walked alone to her apartment.

"Pleasant, indeed. It's wonderful to see you again, Erica."

Randolph broke the moments of silence that followed Rick's words. "Well, we should be on our way, Erica. Bassano is out there waiting to be explored. Rick, we will see you later, since we're all stuck here now." He noticed Erica's puzzled look. "I'll explain later, dear. I mean *cara*."

She released Randolph's arm and gave Rick a soft hug. As he took in her scent, she whispered in Italian.

"Ricky, I must talk to you."

Chapter Five

Betta Innocenti placed a steaming soup bowl in front of Rick before setting another before her father. She was dressed more casually than earlier in the day when he'd dropped in at the gallery, wearing a white apron to give the outfit an even more domestic touch. After putting a bowl at her own place she pulled off the apron and sat down at the table.

"*Buon appetito*, please start. I'm afraid this isn't a very fancy lunch, Riccardo, but my father has to keep his meals simple. Doctor's orders."

"*Un cretino*," Fabio Innocenti grunted, before taking a sip of red wine and picking up his spoon.

The dining room of the Innocenti apartment faced the square, but gray, gauze curtains covered the windows and the view. Since there was no sign of a Signora Innocenti, Rick wondered if the room's feminine touches were thanks to Betta. Given her age, he doubted it. More likely the decoration had been done years earlier and retained for sentimental reasons. Centered prominently on the long crochet runner of the sideboard was a large soup tureen, ornately decorated in a style he had seen in the many ceramics shops of Bassano. The decoration continued with a collection of plates that hung from the walls, and with bowls of different sizes and shapes on a wooden bric-a-brac shelf against one wall. He had only just met Betta, but her look and style did not match those of the ceramics of the room. But her cooking abilities, it appeared, were pleasantly old-fashioned.

"This is wonderful, Betta. *Pasta e fagioli*, am I right?"

"Yes, a Veneto specialty. My mother's recipe." She exchanged glances with her father. "Some people drizzle olive oil. Would you like it?"

"No, no. I want to savor the taste of the beans and the other ingredients you've put in it. A perfect dish for a cool day, especially with this to go with it." He broke off a piece of crusty bread. "It was kind of you to invite me."

"It was my father's idea, Riccardo. He wanted to talk about the missing paintings."

The older man's face wore a slight smile when Rick looked at him, but he immediately turned serious. "Yes, Riccardo, I have some theories on what could be happening, but at this point they are all just that, theories. If there is movement in this case, I see two general possibilities. Both assume that the paintings are in the hands of a private party, and that party wishes to sell them. Most likely they would be bought by another private party, someone wealthy who wishes to have them in his private collection. That's one possibility. Though it could be an institution, but acquiring them would be messy and complicated. A story would have to be created to make the transaction appear legal, and I have no idea how that would be done. But in Italy, such things are possible." He paused to take a spoonful of the *minestra*.

"The only local institution I can think of," Rick said, "would be the museum. Dottor Tibaldi makes no secret of his desire that it be the premier collection of Jacopo da Bassano works in Italy."

Innocenti nodded as he patted his lips with his napkin. "True. But many other museums in Italy would welcome the paintings. *The Accademia*, for example. As you learned in the seminar, Riccardo, the Venetians consider Jacopo one of theirs, despite the painter's insistence on staying in his hometown of Bassano. There are others as well, with more money to spend than our little museum here."

"Father, do you really think a museum would be trying to buy these paintings?"

Innocenti sighed. "I suppose not, Elizabetta, but we have to consider all possibilities." He looked at Rick who had just taken a drink. "Riccardo, how do you like the wine? It is a simple Valpolicella from a winery west of here." He turned to his daughter. "We should have opened something more elegant for our guest, don't you think my dear?"

"This wine is excellent," Rick said quickly before Betta could respond. Considerably better than the half-gallon bottles of Valpolicella in the supermarket in Albuquerque, he thought. Obviously the Italians keep the good stuff for themselves. "Do you still think Muller and Sarchetti are the most likely to be mixed up in this?"

Betta answered for her father. "If you accept the version that the two paintings were carried back to Germany at the end of the war, then Signor Muller would be the logical one to know where they are now. And Sarchetti, as an art dealer with a questionable past—was I supposed to mention that, Father?"

Innocenti shrugged. "I don't see why not. Riccardo has the complete trust of the art police, according to Captain Scuderi." He turned back to Rick. "Apparently Sarchetti's been on their radar for a while for various alleged transgressions."

Rick scraped the last beans from the bowl onto his spoon and slipped it into his mouth. "So it was Sarchetti's appearance at the seminar that sent up the red flags for you, Signor Innocenti?"

"Yes, that was part of it. It seemed logical that the one who has those paintings would show up for a seminar on Jacopo. But maybe it doesn't make any sense at all." He stared at his wineglass in thought.

Betta got to her feet and took her father's empty bowl. "Riccardo, can I get you more *pasta e fagioli*? After this is only cheese and a salad, so—"

"No, thank you, Betta. That was perfect."

She gathered up the other two bowls and disappeared into the kitchen. Her father watched her go and turned to Rick. "I am very proud of my daughter, Riccardo."

Rick was not expecting such a comment. "I'm sure you are, sir."

"When her mother died, she went on to the university, got her degree in fine arts, and came back here to work with me. Without her I…I don't know what I would have done. But her goal is to join the art squad, and I'm not sure I want that for her. It's my own fault, for getting involved on an informal basis, and now she's fascinated by these cases. It's just that—"

Betta returned carrying a bowl of salad greens and a wooden cutting board with a slice of cheese the color of fresh cream. She put both on the table and retrieved a set of small bottles from the sideboard along with six small dishes. In a large soup spoon she poured oil from one of the bottles, added a splash of vinegar from the other, and dashed it with salt before stirring the mixture in the spoon with a fork. Finally the dressing was spooned over the lettuce and gently tossed in the bowl before Betta divided it between the plates. She served her father first and then Rick.

"I've been keeping an eye on Sarchetti." She picked up her fork, a signal that the others could start their salads. "He kept to himself at the seminar, as far as I could tell. The bar in the hotel was his favorite haunt in the evenings, though one afternoon, after the session, he slipped out and visited Signora Bontempi." Innocenti grunted. "She's an elderly woman with a private art collection that has some interesting pieces. Father has been trying to get her to sell some of them for years but she resists."

"She loves the attention of art dealers," Innocenti said, "so she lets the word out that she may be open to parting with some of her pieces. They come, sip some port with her, and leave empty-handed. And not very good port at that. Perhaps when she dies her family will sell."

"Or at least stock better port." Rick scored a smile from both Betta and her father.

After the salad, cheese was passed around with what was left of the bread. The soft asiago, from a dairy run by friends of the Innocentis, went perfectly with the last of the Valpolicella.

"Elizabetta, things are slow at the shop, so why don't you show our guest around the city? You did want to see some of Bassano, didn't you Riccardo?"

"Yes, but I don't want Betta to go to any trouble."

"I have an idea." She stood and gathered the dishes. "It's a perfect day to drive up to Asolo. Have you been there, Riccardo?"

"I have not."

"*Un gioiello.* Fascinating history, a small museum, wonderful views."

"That sounds perfect. I'll go back to the hotel and get my rental car."

"No need, Riccardo, I'll drive."

◇◇◇

Rick had entered from the piazza side of the building when he'd arrived for lunch, was buzzed in at the door, and climbed the tiles steps to the apartment above the gallery. The commute to work could not have been easier for Innocenti and his daughter. Now he followed Betta as she descended a narrow wooden staircase to the street behind the building. At the bottom was a small hallway, what might have been called a mud room in some parts of the States. A door on the interior side led, he assumed, to the shop, and the other to the street. Betta, now dressed in a red leather jacket, reached into a cubby and pulled out two gleaming black helmets. She passed one to Rick, studying his head.

"That should fit you, Riccardo, you look about the same size." She pushed open the door to reveal a black and red motorcycle parked on the cobblestones of the narrow back street. It leaned forward, as if unhappy to be standing still.

Rick turned the helmet in his hands. "You must take people on rides often, Betta, if you have an extra helmet."

"It belongs to the owner. He lets me use his motorcycle while he's away."

"Not just any motorcycle, a Ducati Mostro. He must be a very good friend to do that."

She snapped the chin strap and pulled the dark visor over her face. "He is. He's also my brother. Marco is doing his military service."

Rick was pulling on his helmet, so she might have missed his smile. "Can we fit on this thing?"

"There's only one way to find out, Riccardo." She straddled the seat, inserted a key from her pocket into the column, and the motor came to life with a low panther purr. He snapped his strap and climbed on behind her. There was enough room, but nothing excessive. He found the foot pads and carefully placed his arms around her as the bike moved forward. The sound of the engine bounced off the buildings of the narrow street. How did the neighbors feel about the Innocenti kids owning a motorcycle? To him the throaty roar was not nearly so annoying as the incessant buzzing of small motorbikes in his Roman neighborhood. But urban noise had become a part of him—he almost couldn't get to sleep any more without the comforting din from the streets.

She stopped at the corner and checked both ways before steering from the alley behind the shop onto a wider street. Rick's perch was higher than Betta's, so he had an unobstructed view over the top of her helmet. The street climbed slowly to the eastern edge of the center of town where they stopped for a traffic light, the engine idling with an impatient growl. Betta had the left turn signal on, but as they sat there she called out something and switched it to right.

"What?" shouted Rick over the sound of the Ducati. "I couldn't hear."

"Sarchetti. He just drove by. We'll follow him." She revved the engine, and when the green light appeared they shot off to the right, Rick now holding on for safety as well as pleasure. Sarchetti's car was a silver Alfa Romeo sedan with Milan plates. He was alone. The car moved through the little traffic at the edge of town before heading southwest where houses were farther apart and open fields took over the landscape. Anyone driving this road might think that agriculture was still the mainstay of the Veneto economy, rather than the small businesses and factories that now made it the most prosperous region in Italy, and one of the richest in Europe.

Betta kept a safe distance as Sarchetti speeded up. He slowed only to pass through small towns: Marini, Bessica, Loria, and

Riese Pio X which, Rick read on a sign, had added the name of a local priest when he'd become pope. One of the perks of the office. A moment later they were out amid the fields again, on another straight road. The Alfa speeded up but suddenly slowed down and turned into a small driveway with an open gate. Betta slowed down and passed, while she and Rick watched the car start up the gravel driveway toward a low villa. A hundred meters ahead she decelerated and pulled to the side. They flipped up their darkened visors and looked back at the villa, still visible at the top of the small hill.

"We'll drive by again and get a good look at this place," she called to Rick. She was about to make the U-turn but waited while a dark blue Fiat drove past and disappeared around a bend. She pulled out and the bike purred slowly past the gate. It was closing, either automatically or from someone inside pushing a button.

The villa where Sarchetti's car was now parked could well have been designed by Andrea Palladio, the architect of Bassano's covered bridge. This part of the Veneto was studded with the vacation villas of wealthy sixteenth-century Venetians, and this one looked old enough. Rick was not enough of a student of architecture to recognize it. His eye was drawn to the square, two-story domed center, supported by columns reminiscent of a plantation in the American south. From the core structure, colonnades spread left and right, ending in smaller outbuildings featuring domed roofs that imitated that of the central building. The driveway was protected by low hedges, and it split a wide lawn that ran as far as he could see in both directions. Behind the villa rose a hill covered with large trees, their greens contrasting with the yellow of the building. He guessed that the working parts of the villa, including perhaps pens for animals, were hidden between the villa and the hill, so as not to distract the viewer's eye from its elegant symmetry. The motorcycle followed a bend in the road and the building disappeared from sight. They both lowered their visors back into place as she picked up speed.

"Nice place," Rick shouted. "Any idea who lives there?"

She slowed down, lowering the noise level. "There are so many villas around here, Riccardo, it's hard to keep track of the owners. We'll stop in town and see if we can find out." Within minutes they got back to Riese Pio X. "Let's stop here for a coffee. It may be the best place to get some information." Rick gave a thumbs-up, and she pulled in front of an establishment called Bar Pio X on the main street. Both instinctively ran their fingers through their hair after dismounting and pulling off the helmets. Rick chuckled as he held the door open for Betta.

"What's so funny?"

"I have a good friend from the university back in America who graduated from a school named St. Pius X. I wonder how he'd feel about a place in the pope's hometown called Bar Pius X?"

"But I've heard that a bar in America is not the same as a bar in Italy."

"True, but he wouldn't know that."

It was a typical Italian bar, with a few tables on one side, and a long counter on the other. Tall bottles with strange shapes and decorations ran along the shelves behind the counter, looking like no one had dared to take a drink from them in years. Old men, and no women, sat at one of the tables playing cards, none of them smoking. The yellow tint on the ceiling was a reminder of when cigarettes were not just allowed but encouraged. Rick and Betta walked to the bar where a woman in a white apron sat on a stool staring at the screen of a small TV hanging from one corner. It was black and white, which fit with the rest of the room, and the program Rick guessed was a soap opera.

"*Due caffè, per favore,*" he said.

The woman pulled her attention from the TV, stood, and took two small cups from a shelf next to the espresso machine. As they watched, she placed them under the double spigot of the machine, pulled off the handle above it, filled the filter with brown coffee and slapped it back into place. Soon the water was hissing and dripping through the coffee, becoming a dark brown liquid. Still glancing every few moments at the TV, she put the half-filled cups on their saucers and placed them in front of her two customers before positioning a large sugar bowl between them. Rick noticed that Betta took her espresso without sugar. He added two spoonfuls to his cup.

"Excuse me, Signora," said Betta. "Just before we came into town we noticed a beautiful villa on the right. Is it a Palladio?"

The woman sighed, finally accepting that she would not be able to give full attention to her TV program. She squinted in thought. "That would likely be Villa Berti. Not a Palladio, but I don't know who built it. The new owners had it renovated a couple years ago before moving in. It took forever to complete the work."

Betta exchanged a glance with Rick. "Who owns it now? Must be someone with a lot of euros."

"That's for sure. It's some businessman, owns a few factories in the area. It seems like every day somebody's building a new factory. More than one farmer around here is selling his land for a small fortune, then sitting around all day counting his money. It beats working in the fields, I suppose." She looked at the men playing cards. "Not them, of course. They're just regular pensioners. One coffee when they come in, and then they sit there all afternoon."

"Do you know the name of the owner?" Rick asked. "We're architecture students and thought there might be a way to see it inside."

The woman frowned and took their empty coffee cups. "Doubt if they'd let you in. The man's name is Rinaldi. You could try, I guess."

"Thanks," Betta said, "we just may." She looked at Rick. "Shall we be on our way? Riccardo, are you all right?"

He snapped his attention to Betta. "Yes, yes, I'm fine." He pulled change from his pocket, left it on the counter, and thanked the woman behind it.

Later, as the noise of the engine once again made conversation impossible, Rick returned to his thoughts. The woman at the bar had said the villa owner's name was Rinaldi. His friend Beppo had an uncle who lived in the area, a businessman like

Beppo's father and many others in the family. Could it be that Sarchetti was calling on Beppo Rinaldi's uncle? If so, an art dealer with a shady reputation was meeting with the uncle of a man who works for the art squad and happens to be his close friend. *Wonderful.*

Rick squeezed his arms a bit tighter around Betta's thin waist. Despite the visor covering his face he managed to catch a trace of her still unidentified perfume, taking his mind off Beppo's uncle.

Chapter Six

A group of elderly German tourists stood along the northern side of the bridge, posing for a picture taken by a tour guide who was as young as they were old. It was not raining, nor did the sky threaten any showers, but all the women wore raincoats. They had been told to expect rain, so why pack more than one overcoat? The wood beams of the bridge roof formed the top frame of the photograph, but the mountains were still visible in the distance. Nice photo, Rick thought as he watched the group. It will take a place of honor over their fireplaces in Frieburg or wherever they're from.

Rick thought how pleasantly quaint it was that the guide was using a real camera, rather than a cell phone, to take the picture. He checked his own cell phone for time and messages before slipping it back into his coat. If she didn't show up in another five minutes, he'd gladly be on his way. No, relieved to be on his way. He'd sensed that the urgency of Erica's whispered plea had nothing to do with the two issues that concerned him most at the moment: the murder and the missing paintings. Of course she was engaged to one of the suspects, who gave a vague answer to the question about where he was the previous afternoon. Now that would be something if she had some incriminating information about Randolph. No, that's not going to happen.

"Ricky!"

Erica walked briskly toward him, her long coat flapping open to show the same tight jeans she'd worn in the morning. He watched her approach, trying to decipher the look on her face. Agitation for sure, but what else could he read from it? When she reached him she stopped and took a deep breath before taking his arm and stepping to the wooden railing. They looked down at the water before she spoke again.

"Thank you for meeting me, Ricky. I don't know what to do, and when I saw you it was like being tossed a lifeline."

She spoke in Italian, as they always had. Her voice was steady but tense. It wasn't the voice of an angry Erica; he knew that one well. Something in the way she spoke made him less annoyed, more forgiving. Of course there had been no "How are you, Ricky, how is your business doing, how's your uncle," anything like that. But it was Erica, after all.

"Tell me what's wrong. Perhaps I can help."

"That's just it, I don't know if anything's wrong. I think I'm happy, who wouldn't be? Jeffrey is a wonderful man, I should be the happiest woman in the world, but somehow…"

A long branch dislodged itself from one of the pontoons below them and pushed its way back into the main flow of the river. They watched it catch in the current and disappear into the distance. Her comments confirmed that this was not about murder or lost paintings. As he should have suspected, it was about Erica.

"Start at the beginning." He used his best Dr. Phil manner. "How did you meet Jeff?"

"He was—well, still is—the head of the department. When I arrived to start the lectureship he took me under his wing, made sure I was introduced to the rest of the faculty, made me feel at home. I didn't think much of it at first. I assumed that it was the way any department head in America would welcome a new member of the faculty. Of course his reputation in the art scholarship community was well known to me, it was one of the reasons I applied for the position." For the first time since they'd been standing at the rail she turned and looked at him. "He's one of the top scholars in our field, Ricky."

"Go on." He was already forming his opinion of the problem.

"Jeffrey had been divorced for about a year when I arrived, and when he was helping me get settled we spent a lot of time together, and we became friends as well as colleagues."

"And then it became more than just friendship."

She was back to watching the river. "Yes. But not in the way you might think, Ricky. Jeffrey is very…let's say formal, even old-fashioned."

Rick didn't want to know that level of detail. "The important question, Erica, is if you feel the same way about him as he feels about you. I've spoken to him, and the man is completely smitten. Is it reciprocal?"

"That's the problem, Ricky, I'm not sure. He's sweet, loving, very intelligent…what more could a woman want?"

And he's the head of the department, Rick thought.

"And when I saw you this morning—"

"This isn't about me, Erica."

"I know, I know. But somehow seeing you brought back doubts about whether I am doing the right thing."

I don't need this, Rick thought. I was quite happy to have Erica out of my life, thousands of miles away on another continent. But she needs some help and I can't just brush her off, as much as I'd like to. Too bad she doesn't have a girlfriend to help her deal with this decision, but Erica was never one to have close girlfriends in Rome, and she likely didn't make any close female friendships in the States. That would be the day. OK, she wants to marry the guy and be the wife of the famous scholar, but needs a push. Why not give her that push?

"Erica, I've been very impressed by Jeff."

"You did his translation, Ricky, you know how good he is in his field."

"Yes, that of course, but also he seems like a very decent guy. Personable, pleasant to be around. It's your decision, mind you, but I don't see why…" He couldn't quite bring himself to finish the sentence.

She kissed him lightly on the cheek. "You're very sweet, Ricky. I'd better get back to the hotel. Jeffrey was checking his e-mail and I said I was going to take a short walk. I didn't tell him that—"

"Of course. That wasn't necessary."

He watched her leave the bridge and walk up the hill out of sight. The sound of her heels was covered by the chatter of the German tourists, but her perfume still lingered in the air. Had he done the right thing? Said the right words? Was what he said sufficiently neutral to support the decision she finally made? He sighed and looked at the buildings along the eastern side of the river, their windows lit by the afternoon sun. The ceramics museum occupied one of those *palazzi* that overlooked the water and he wondered if there was time to check it out before dinner. He was disappointed that the trip to Asolo hadn't happened, but Betta wanted to return to report to her father on tailing Sarchetti. The thought of her made him smile. He was pleased that she'd immediately accepted his invitation to dinner. She should suggest a place, somewhere that Jeff and Erica would not know about.

His phone rang and he fumbled in his jacket to find it. Not a number he knew.

"Montoya."

"Riccardo, this is Angelo Rinaldi, Beppo's uncle…Hello?

Rick regained his voice. "Yes, sir." He looked up at the beams in the roof of the bridge, gathering his thoughts.

"Beppo called me to say that his good friend Riccardo Montoya is in Bassano, so I was calling to see if we can get together. My nephew spoke very highly of you, Riccardo."

"That is very kind of him, and of you, Signor Rinaldi, but you must be a busy man."

"Not too busy to extend my hospitality to a friend of Beppo. I know it is late, but could you come to dinner this evening? I live not too far outside of town."

"I was going to have dinner with a friend here in—"

"*Perfetto*. You shall bring her along. I trust it is a young lady, Riccardo. Beppo told me you have an eye for beauty, and not just in Etruscan funerary sculpture."

◇◇◇

This time they drove in Rick's rental, an Alfa Romeo Giulietta he had picked up at the Villa Borghese rental agency in Rome. The car's dark exterior matched the coffee color of Betta's long skirt, with both paint and cloth complementing their respective chassis. She had worn minimal makeup during the day, but when he picked her up that evening in front of the shop she had a soft blush on her face which contrasted with the dark hair and darker eyes. She gave him a peck on the cheek and slipped into the seat of the Alfa. Rick closed the passenger door carefully and walked around to the driver's side while trying again to identify her perfume. He would have to ask. It was his experience that women loved being asked about their perfume.

"This should be an interesting evening," she said as Rick pulled slowly from the curb. "I feel like we're going undercover." She flashed a quick smile.

You don't know the half of it, he thought. "Likely it's just a coincidence, and the man is without blemish, but it is somewhat eerie that we actually followed someone to his villa this very afternoon."

"Isn't it? His nephew, your friend, what does he do in Rome? Also a businessman, I suppose?"

"He should be an industrialist, like his father and his uncle, but Beppo works in an office at the Culture Ministry. Is this where I turn?"

After a few traffic lights, on the same route they had taken earlier, the buildings became fewer and the only lights were from their headlights and the occasional farmhouse along the side of the road. The few cars they passed were coming toward Bassano, likely for a meal in one of the city's restaurants. The farther they drove from town the fewer the cars in either direction.

Betta turned in her seat and looked at Rick's profile. "Do you always wear your hair this long?"

"It's not really that long." He took one hand off the wheel and ran it through his hair while he tried to remember the last time he'd been to the barber. "You think I should cut it?"

"No, no. It looks fine. It goes with the cowboy boots." She turned her eyes back to the road ahead. "It's the first time I've been out with a man who wears cowboy boots."

"Back in New Mexico, all the women I dated wore cowboy boots."

"Really?"

"You should get a pair. You'd be surprised how comfortable they are."

"And I imagine they protect you against rattlesnakes."

"That too."

The road was now a straight line. They watched a set of headlights appear in the distance, get larger, and zip past them. "Is it really that different in America?"

Rick glanced at Betta and then back at the pavement. "If you're hoping I'll say that people are the same under the skin the world over, you'll be disappointed. Do you think that Milanese are different from Neapolitans?"

"They're not from the same planet."

"And proud of it."

"So how is your New Mexico different from my Veneto?"

"To begin with, the women here ask harder questions."

Ten minutes later their car turned into the driveway and stopped at the gate. "Signor Montoya?" squawked a voice from an invisible source.

"*Si,*" Rick called through his open window as he searched unsuccessfully for a camera or microphone. The gate ground open and they drove up the gravel driveway to the house, where a man in a white coat came down the steps and opened the car door to allow Betta to step out.

"You may leave the car where it is, Signor Montoya. There is only one other guest this evening." He nodded toward a dark sedan parked a few meters in front of Rick's car. "This way, please." Rick and Betta followed him up a few steps, where he held open the door for them to enter the villa and then closed it behind them. "May I take your wrap, Signora?"

"I'll keep it for the moment, thank you." The garment over her shoulders, a milky coffee color, was something between a scarf and a shawl. It hung loosely over a silk blouse, the corners almost reaching the top of the long skirt. Rick wore the same suit and tie from the previous evening's festivities, if the dinner could now be called that after Fortuna's murder, and his more formal pair of cowboy boots.

The round entrance hall mirrored the central dome which both Rick and Betta instinctively turned their heads up to see. It had been painted blue, with a few white wisps of cloud and a passing bird, the entire sky lit by lights hidden around the lower edge. The man waited patiently while they looked, then showed them into a room beyond the hallway decorated with stuffed furniture, side tables, and ceramic lamps. The chairs and sofas were arranged into two conversation areas, but both faced a fireplace that ran from floor to ceiling. Rick guessed that, as old as the villa might be, the fireplace had been brought from some more ancient structure. Its opening was large enough to allow someone to stand upright inside it and still survey the room. Above its high mantle a coat of arms featuring a lion and three half-moons was carved into the stone. Four tall glass doors dominated the left wall. They would offer a spectacular view of the lawn and distant hills in daytime, but now only the covered walkway was visible.

Angelo Rinaldi stood in front of the fireplace where a few logs glowed, a glass in his hand. He wore a herringbone jacket with a paisley tie, the picture of the country gentleman. A closely cropped goatee made it difficult for Rick to discern any resemblance between Rinaldi and his nephew, but perhaps when he got closer it would show.

The other guest sat in the middle of a large sofa, glass in hand, looking up at the host. Rick guessed her age to be mid forties, about a decade younger than Rinaldi but in no rush to show it. Her dress was classic black, sleeveless and cut just enough below the neck to display a simple gold chain and pearl pendant. Her hem hovered tastefully just above the knee where her left hand rested. Rinaldi put down his glass and walked quickly toward Rick and Betta, weaving through the bulky furniture along the way. The woman stayed seated, an aloof smile on her lips.

"Riccardo, I'm so glad you could come this evening." He shook Rick's hand and turned to Betta. "And this *bella creatura?*"

"Elizabetta Innocenti, Signor Rinaldi, but she prefers Betta."

The man kissed Betta's hand with a practiced flair. "And Betta it will be, but you shall both call me Angelo. I insist. Come, meet my other guest." As they walked toward her, the woman took a sip from her drink, set it down, and brushed back a bit of her hair that had fallen over her eyebrows. She stood and inclined her head while studying Rick. "Caterina, this is Riccardo Montoya, the good friend of my nephew. Riccardo, Caterina Savona." They shook hands. "And this is Rick's friend Betta Innocenti."

Was there a faint twinge in the face of the woman when she was introduced to Betta? After the introductions, the woman insisted on sitting with Betta while her host stood with Rick. The man who had ushered them into the room reappeared with two thin glasses of prosecco. After serving Rick and Betta, and assuring himself that the others didn't need refills, he disappeared through the doorway. Rinaldi called out a brief toast to the ladies—already deep in conversation—and turned back to Rick. They stood in front of the fireplace, its fire sending out the faint smell of a wood Rick couldn't place. He was sure only that it wasn't the piñon pine he remembered from winter nights in New Mexico.

"Beppo spoke very highly of you, Riccardo. Said you had been very helpful in some case of his, but didn't go into detail." Rinaldi noticed Rick glancing at Betta. "No, I won't mention Beppo's profession to your lady friend, I sense that you have not either."

"No, I haven't. It didn't seem relevant."

Rinaldi chuckled. "I suppose not. And what does she do?"

"She and her father have an art gallery in Bassano." Rick glanced around him, noticing paintings of various sizes and styles on the walls. "Perhaps you've been to it."

"I don't purchase my art locally. I use dealers in Milan and Zurich, and one in London." He sipped his prosecco. "They know my tastes."

"And Signora Savona? What brings her to Bassano?"

"Not just to see me, I will admit, but I'm pleased that she's here." He looked at the two women conversing on the sofa and back at Rick. His voice lowered slightly. "I must confess to you, Riccardo, that I am the black sheep of the *famiglia* Rinaldi." Rick's eyes narrowed and the man continued. "Nothing that serious, I assure you, but I've never married and my siblings find this shocking. I've had the opportunity, of course, and was even tempted to tie the knot a few times, but never succumbed. I justify a lifestyle that my family considers satyric, supported by a firm belief that they would be more upset if I had married and then divorced." He looked again at the women before turning back to Rick. "But I have not answered your question. Caterina is in the art field, though I'm not sure exactly what part of it. A mutual acquaintance alerted me to her arrival from Milan today—just as with you, Riccardo—so I took the opportunity to ask her to join us. She is a delightful woman."

When the *maggiordomo* announced that dinner was ready to be served, Rinaldi offered his arm to Betta and Rick followed suit with Caterina Savona.

"You work very fast, Riccardo," she said softly in his ear. "Betta tells me you two met only this morning."

"It's been a busy day. Are you staying here at the villa?"

She gave his arm a playful pinch. "Heavens, no, I'm just here for dinner. I'm staying in town at the Belvedere."

"That's where I am. A very pleasant hotel."

"So I've heard, which is why I chose it."

The dining room was on the same wing, with another set of doors on one side looking out on the colonnade. Lights between the outdoor columns lit the stone walkway and spilled out onto the first few meters of grass. In the darkness faint twinkles hinted of another villa or farm in the distance. Rick was expecting a large room with a long table, but instead it was considerably smaller than the living room and had only a sideboard and round glass table set for four. Perhaps there was a banquet room further down the wing. As in the other room, the ceiling was lined with dark wood beams, likely the originals. Decorative pole lamps in the corners threw light upward, the only lighting other than four candles in an arrangement at the center of the table. The gentlemen held out the chairs for the ladies and everyone was seated.

Rinaldi took his napkin from the plate and spread it on his lap. "Since Caterina and Riccardo are not from the Veneto, I thought we would have some regional specialties. I hope you won't mind, Betta."

She had Rick on her left and the host on her right. "Absolutely not, Signor—excuse me, Angelo—we must show these *stranieri* what they are missing."

Rinaldi beamed. "And *vino locale* too, of course, starting off with a Breganze produced just to our west, a smooth Pinot Bianco." As if on cue the butler appeared, and after the host had gone through a cursory tasting, filled the glasses of the two women, followed by those of the men. The four toasted and sipped the straw yellow wine.

"Excellent," said Caterina. "I will have to look for it at my wine shop in Milano." She put down her glass and turned her eyes to Rinaldi. "Angelo, you have the reputation of a discriminating collector of art. Tell us what you are looking at these days. Collectors are always thinking about their next acquisition, you must be the same."

"My dear, you are correct in characterizing the collector, but at the moment I am concentrating on business." Rick and Betta exchanged quick glances, unnoticed by the other two. "We are considering expanding into a new line, and it's been consuming my attention. But I'll get back to art soon enough. Once you have the itch…" The first course arrived in individual bowls, rice dotted with peas and pieces of *pancetta* sprinkled with parsley. Rick recognized it to be a dish he'd tasted as a kid on a school trip to Venice. Rinaldi confirmed it. "*Risi e bisi* should be thick, but not too thick, and of course the rice and peas must be perfectly *al dente. Buon appetito.*"

The conversation turned naturally to food, specifically rice dishes. Caterina told the group about the history of *risotto alla milanese*, how rich Milanesi in the middle ages actually used gold dust to color the rice. Though no one at the table had ever tasted gold, they all agreed that saffron likely provided a better flavoring. Rick admitted that rice balls filled with cheese and fried, *supplì di riso*, were one of his favorite antipasto dishes, and went on to describe the delicious simplicity of the beans and rice he'd had when visiting his parents in Brazil. It was while the dishes of the first course were being removed that Rinaldi changed the subject.

"Riccardo, it was that seminar on Jacopo da Bassano where you were working as an interpreter, wasn't it?"

"Yes, it was. An interesting topic, I learned a great deal about the man and his times."

Rinaldi inclined his head toward the empty bottle and the butler, removing the last bowl, nodded in recognition before walking toward the door. "The bank sponsored it, if I remember right from the posters I saw around town. Stefano Porcari was probably behind it." He turned to the lady on his left. "Stefano is the vice president of the Banco di Bassano, Caterina, and very much interested in art."

"Have you ever considered collecting from that period, Angelo?" It was Betta. "Jacopo or one of his contemporaries."

The girl's got spunk, Rick thought. He waited for Rinaldi's reply, but it was interrupted by the need to taste a newly opened bottle. It was a red, this time, almost garnet in color.

"No, my dear, I think Jacopo is a bit too dear for an amateur collector like me. Of course I would love to have something by our most famous local son, but his work is likely out of my price range. Not that they come on the market that often, of course." He watched the butler fill everyone's second wineglass. "The grapes for this Montello were grown not ten kilometers from where we are seated, by a good friend. I'm afraid it is not one that you will find in your wine shop in Milano, Caterina. *Salute.*"

The butler appeared again from the kitchen, this time accompanied by a woman dressed in a white apron. Each carried a platter in one hand and a serving spoon in the other. Going first to the ladies, the butler placed a small half bird on each plate, then stepped aside so that a spoonful of roasted potatoes could be placed next to it.

When everyone was served the master of the house waved a hand asking them to begin eating. "Pigeon is usually thought of as a specialty of Umbria, something which I've always found curious, given that it was the home of Saint Francis, but these stuffed pigeons are a Veneto tradition. I hope you'll enjoy them."

Rick discovered that the bird had been conveniently split in half, allowing easy access to a ham, breading, and herb filling inside. There was little meat, but what there was fell easily off the bone into its own juice. The crunchy potatoes contrasted deliciously with the savory flavors of the pigeon. "This is a splendid meal, Angelo." He raised his glass. "Our compliments and thanks to your cook."

"One of the best in the Veneto, Riccardo." He joined his guests in another sip of the Montello. "To return to the seminar, if I may. I heard on the local TV news before you arrived that one of the participants was killed last night. Do you know about that, Riccardo?"

From the look on Caterina Savona's face, it appeared that this was the first she had heard of it. Betta looked at Rick, awaiting his reply.

"Professor Fortuna, one of the specialists in all things Jacopo. He met his end last night after our final dinner for the panelists, organizers, and sponsors. It was quite a shock this morning to everyone, as you might imagine, when the police descended on the hotel."

"It certainly would be a shock," Caterina said in a halting voice. "What do they think happened?"

"I really couldn't say. They questioned all of us, of course, and we've been told to stay put for the moment. Which is going to inconvenience some of the participants."

"Who were the other participants, Riccardo?" Betta's question, Rick knew, was intended to draw out their host. The wine and food had not diverted her from the mission.

"There are three foreign specialists. Jeffrey Randolph is from a university in America. George Oglesby is similarly employed in England. And Karl Muller is a German who is apparently quite a Jacopo specialist. Among the Italians, besides the late Lorenzo Fortuna, was Taddeo Gaddi, another university professor, and the curator of the Jacopo collection at the museum, Dottor Tibaldi."

"I've met Tibaldi," said Rinaldi. "Knows his art, but you would expect that from someone in his position."

Rick caught Betta's eye and then continued. "There were a few other people who weren't on the panels but participated to a certain extent. Some graduate students...oh, and there was a man from Milan named Sarchetti. Art dealer."

Rinaldi's face showed nothing. "From Milan? Do you know him, Caterina?"

She grasped her wineglass. "I recall hearing the name."

"But do the police have any leads, Riccardo? It would seem to me that a group of art historians would not be the best pool for finding a murder suspect. Perhaps some enemy of the man followed him here and did him in. I trust that the usual robbery gone bad theory has been floated?"

Rick put down his fork. "The police will probably tell you that they are not ruling anything out. That's their usual statement, isn't it?"

"Which usually means," Caterina said, "that they have no idea what happened."

"Well, I hope they find out quickly who did it. We don't need an investigation dragging on. But as your host I should not have brought up such a subject, I prefer to discuss more enjoyable topics. Such as art." He turned to Rick. "We are in the presence of two women who know their art. I would love to get their opinion on something which must have come up at the conference, Riccardo—those two lost Jacopo paintings. Here in Bassano, they are considered part of our city's patrimony."

Rick tried not to show any reaction. "Definitely discussed. I had never heard of them, so I found it all fascinating."

"What I've heard," Betta interjected, "is that they are hidden in some cave, or stashed away in the home of a wealthy collector. Have you hidden them in one of the rooms here, Angelo?"

She gave the host a sly wink, and Rick wondered if the wine was finally having an effect on her. Rinaldi laughed. "I wish that were the case, my dear. Caterina, have you heard about these paintings in your travels?"

Caterina Savona had been watching the exchange, and thought for a moment before replying. "Yes. If I remember the story, they disappeared at the end of the war, so wouldn't that increase the likelihood that they were spirited out of Italy altogether? They could be hidden in plain sight on the wall of some German house without the owner even knowing how valuable they are. Such things can happen. There was a famous case of a missing Caravaggio turning up in someone's basement years ago."

"I will search my basement first thing in the morning," said Rinaldi. The dishes from the second course had been cleared during the conversation, and he returned to the subject of food. "For dessert we have the most famous of our local dishes, *tiramisú*, created just down the road in Treviso. It has been imitated throughout the world, most often with disastrous results, but it remains a classic. In London last year I was forced by good manners to have one that bore no resemblance to the dish you will savor now."

"That's quite an introduction, Angelo."

"And well deserved, Caterina, thanks to my wonderful cook. So, do you think these paintings will ever appear?"

"My opinion is worth nothing, but I would wager that they will never be found. If the person who has them does not know their value, the paintings will likely stay put. And if they do know they have masterpieces, they probably know how they got there, and want to keep anyone from finding out."

No one had anything to add, and they were rescued by the arrival of dessert.

◇◇◇

"He didn't even blink when you mentioned Sarchetti."

Rick drove slowly along the two-lane road. The Alfa's headlights reflected off the kilometer markers, and at intersections they picked up rectangular signs pointing the way to small towns in this part of the valley. Clouds had spread over the area while they'd been in the villa, blotting out the stars and any glimpse of a moon, as well as hinting of rain. As they went through Riese, rain became reality, though the drops were not enough to require the wipers.

"He never said he didn't know the man," Rick replied. "It was a clever response. Still, we can't dismiss the possibility that Sarchetti was visiting the butler this afternoon. Or getting some recipe from the cook. It was, you must admit, an excellent *tiramisú*."

Rick could not make out her face in the darkened car, but from her next comment he sensed that Betta wasn't smiling. "And Caterina said she'd only heard of Sarchetti, whatever that meant, before the subject was conveniently changed by our gracious host."

Caterina and Angelo must be in cahoots, Rick thought. As happened so often in his line of work, he began to consider translations for the phrase "in cahoots," as well as possible origins. He would have to look it up when he got back to the hotel, since the wine and rich food weren't allowing his mind to work as it should. A bright light flashed in the rearview mirror, taking his mind off etymology. They had passed few cars since leaving the villa, and none had passed them. But this driver acted anxious to do so. Already going under the speed limit, if there was one at this time of night on Italian roads, Rick slowed down even more, expecting the driver to roar past. Instead, the lights came almost to Rick's bumper.

"What's he doing?" Betta craned to look back.

"I don't know, but I don't like it." Rick instinctively accelerated to get away from the car, but it stayed glued to theirs. What came to his mind was a defensive driving course his father had taken once to get away from a possible kidnapper, something about slamming on the hand brake while shifting the steering wheel to make a sudden turn. He doubted it would work on a narrow road at night, a road now getting slicker with the rain. He fumbled to find the wiper knob.

"Should we stop?" There was fear in Betta's voice.

"That may be exactly what he wants. Let's see what this Alfa Romeo can do." He stomped on the gas pedal and the car shot forward. It took a moment, but eventually the lights matched Rick's speed. Far ahead, through thickening drops of rain, he could see the lights of a town. If they could get there...

Now larger lights appeared ahead of him. It was impossible to know how fast they were coming at him but they seemed high. Perhaps a truck. Rick tensed when he looked in his mirror to find that the car following him was speeding up to pass. Didn't the driver see the truck coming? The car barely reached past Rick's front bumper when it squeezed right to cut him off.

"Riccardo, look out!"

There was nowhere to go but off the pavement. Rick wanted to see who was in the car, but he had to concentrate on the road, or what was left of it. He hit the brake, swerving toward the shoulder as the large oncoming truck blared its horn. By braking, the Alfa skidded sideways, its tires sending rough shudders through the entire vehicle. The steering wheel vibrated in Rick's hands but he managed to turn into the slide and regained control. The Alfa skewed off the road and thumped down an embankment, stopping short of a wire fence as the engine sputtered and died. The other car shot past the oncoming truck, its tail lights disappearing into the darkness. They sat for a moment without speaking.

"*Stai bene?*" He put his hand on hers. "You're shaking."

"A little, but I'm all right now. What was the matter with that guy?"

"I don't know. Let's get out of this ditch. Luckily it's not that deep." He turned the key to bring the Alfa back to life. The wheels spun slightly before gripping and moving the car slowly back to the shoulder and then into the road. Rick stopped and opened the window to take a gulp of the fresh air, but instead he smelled the diesel exhaust of the truck now gone behind them. It was silent, the only sound the purr of the car's engine. The whole incident, he realized, took no more than a couple minutes. Who was it? As his pulse slowed down he couldn't help thinking that it was not a drunken driver or being in the wrong place at the wrong time. For one thing, there was something familiar about the car. Even in the darkness he could tell that its paint was dark, probably black or dark blue. A Fiat? Not sure, since cars often look alike. Perhaps something would eventually come to mind. He squeezed Betta's hand and took a deep breath before putting the car into gear. A quiet twenty minutes later he drove into the deserted piazza and parked in front of the store.

He turned off the ignition and took her hand in both of his. "Not the excitement we needed to end the evening, Betta. Are you sure you're all right?"

She put her other hand over his. "Can you come up for a few minutes? I don't want to be alone yet. I can make us coffee."

"Your father won't still be up?"

She smiled. "He may be, but I live in the apartment across the hall."

He got out and walked around to open her door. When her shoe touched the pavement he remembered where he had seen the car.

Chapter Seven

Rick stifled a yawn as he perused the inner pages of *La Repubblica*, not sure if it was the political news from Rome or the lack of sleep that had caused it. He'd turned the key to his hotel room door well after midnight, but an hour or two less in bed hadn't kept him from his morning run. Bassano's fresh air filling his lungs each morning had invigorated his trip. Even though he ran early in the morning in Rome, before the worst traffic took over the streets, he couldn't escape the fumes that lingered there. Only when it had rained during the night, or a strong wind had blown through, did Roman air take on a quality approaching freshness. He folded his paper, dropped a couple euro coins on the table, and walked to the lobby.

Now that's interesting.

In the far corner of the room, where he had seen Inspector Occasio talking with the banker the previous morning, sat Caterina Savona. Her outfit was more informal than the previous evening: a short jacket covered a turtleneck sweater, slacks and boots completing the outfit. Her hair was in the same style as at dinner, but combed out. "Businesslike," was the word that came to his mind. As he watched, she and the man she'd been talking with stood and shook hands, a formal handshake as if they just met. The man's double-breasted jacket was tailored to disguise the size of his stomach, but a certain amount of neck hanging over the shirt collar spoiled the effect. His hair was as

Rick remembered it from looking through the window of his translator's booth: disheveled and in need of a cut. The fellow tried to cut the figure of a neat person despite a few too many pounds, but didn't quite pull it off. Why was he talking with Caterina Savona?

Rick walked to the elevator and was about to press the call button when he heard a familiar voice behind him.

"*Buon giorno*, Riccardo."

"*Buon giorno*, Caterina. Nice to see you again."

"*Altretanto*. I so enjoyed meeting you and Betta. You make a lovely couple."

Rick almost returned the compliment, but opted against it. Instead he let his curiosity get the best of him. "I didn't recall your saying last night that you knew Sarchetti."

She glanced back at where they'd been sitting. "You are very observant, Riccardo. In fact I hadn't met him, but since his name came up at dinner I made a point of doing so this morning. We are both in the art business."

"I never heard exactly what part of that business you're in." Was the smile on her face forced or genuine?

"Buying and selling is what I'm involved in, Riccardo, like Franco Sarchetti."

"I wouldn't think the arts community is that large in Milano. You hadn't met him before?"

"I've only recently moved to Milan from Rome, so I'm getting to know the players. Your questions make you sound like a policeman, Riccardo." She turned and walked away.

The Museo Civico di Bassano del Grappa was one of the oldest city museums in the Veneto region, dating to 1828 when a local natural history scholar donated his collection to the city. Over the decades it grew from plants and animals to include archeology, sculpture, and painting, as well as its extensive collection of Jacopo da Bassano. The museum was blessed with a building that was a work of art in itself, the ex-convent of Saint Francis.

Rick and Betta sat at a stone bench at the edge of its cloister, enjoying the open square of sky and grass.

"Why didn't you tell me last night, Riccardo?"

"You were so upset I didn't want to add to it."

Two boys from a school group ran out into the perfectly manicured grass to peer into a round, stone well at one corner. One whispered something and the other giggled. Their teacher called out and the two scurried back under the cloister roof.

"You probably did the right thing." She watched the kids march into the main part of the museum. "You are sure that the car was the one that passed us when we stopped to look at the villa yesterday?"

He held up a hand. "I didn't say I was sure. There are a lot of dark sedans in Italy, and especially here in the Veneto. But that's my hunch."

"And when we were stopped, with our visors up, the driver recognized us—"

"Likely me." No need to alarm her more, he thought.

"Recognized one of us, and then followed us that evening. But why?"

"I'd love to know. In the afternoon he could have been following Sarchetti, and we got in the way."

"Then why would he care about where we were going for dinner?"

He shrugged. "Your mentioning Sarchetti reminds me. I ran into Caterina in the lobby this morning."

"Just getting back to the hotel?" She chuckled. "Sorry, that was not nice."

Rick forced a frown. "Certainly not. But the interesting thing was that she was chatting with Sarchetti."

Betta's eyes widened, making them even more attractive. "But she said last night…"

"She came up to me while I was waiting for the elevator. I asked her about it, and she said that after learning Sarchetti was in town, she made a point of meeting him. I believe her. I think."

"There's something very strange about that woman, Riccardo."

"Mysterious is the word I would use." He got to his feet. "Except for one private viewing of the Jacopo collection, I never got out of the conference room during the seminar, so I'm looking forward to seeing the rest of the museum with your guidance. I've never had a museum guide whose beauty matched the artwork on the walls."

She took his arm. "You do have a way with words, Riccardo."

"It's my life's work, Betta."

They entered a long corridor. Paintings hung on both walls, those on one side positioned between the rectangular, curtained windows which looked out on the cloister. Rick pictured nuns walking the corridor when it was a convent, whispering prayers with beads in their hands, an occasional crucifix hanging from the walls rather than brightly colored paintings.

Betta gestured toward the walls. "This section holds paintings of the sixteenth century, including several by Jacopo's sons. The religious themes are typical of the period, and similar to the style of the master."

"His sons copied him."

"Derivative is the term art historians use. Doesn't sound as harsh."

They were viewing one of the larger paintings when a man entered the corridor and stepped rapidly along it deep in thought. His eyes followed the tiled floor rather than the paintings. When he got to the two visitors he looked up and paused.

"Riccardo. I didn't know you were coming to the museum today—you should have asked for me." He shook hands with Rick.

"Dottor Tibaldi, I didn't want to be a nuisance, we're just playing tourists. This is my friend Betta Innocenti. Betta, Dottor Tibaldi is the curator of the museum and was the organizer of the seminar where I interpreted." Another handshake was exchanged.

"Why don't you come into my office for a moment? Then I'll let you get back to your tourism."

Along the hall and up a flight of stairs they passed through a "staff only" door and eventually to a room overlooking the courtyard. Rick wondered if it had once belonged to the mother superior, but didn't ask. Two paintings with a religious theme hung on one wall, a newly framed poster for the seminar on another. The desk was metal and glass. Tibaldi invited them to sit in two of the modern leather chairs arranged in one corner of the room. Modern furniture was virtually a requirement for any office in Italy inside an ancient building. The curator offered coffee which they politely declined. He sat, unbuttoned his suit jacket, and turned to Betta.

"Are you new to Bassano, too, like Riccardo?"

"No, in fact I live here."

Tibaldi squinted his eyes. "You do look familiar. Could we have met before?"

"I come to the museum often."

"Excellent. First and foremost our museum is for the residents of the city. But of course we welcome outside visitors, Riccardo. You have recovered from the seminar? I can't imagine how exhausting interpretation must be."

"That's why we insist on having at least two of us so we can take breaks. The seminar went well, Dottore, from your point of view?"

Tibaldi leaned back and steepled his fingers together. "Unquestionably. The museum can't stand still, it must constantly demonstrate its relevance, not only to the city but also to the arts community in general."

The man was sounding like some of the university fund-raisers Rick had known in Albuquerque. "What are your future plans?" he asked, "to demonstrate that relevance."

"Continuing to be the foremost center for the study of local artists, as this seminar demonstrated. And expanding our collection of works is paramount."

"Including the acquisition of more paintings by Jacopo da Bassano?"

Tibaldi's face showed that Betta's question took him by surprise, but he quickly recovered. "Unfortunately, there are few Jacopos on the market, if any, Signora Innocenti."

"But Riccardo mentioned hearing about some missing works. What about them?"

Once again Betta's technique impressed Rick. He couldn't have asked that question, but with a smile as innocent as her name, she pulled it off.

Tibaldi cleared his throat before answering. "It is unfortunate that some of the precious time in the seminar was devoted to paintings that have not been seen for decades, and unfortunately may be destroyed, rather than concentrating on known works such as those in our collection."

"It was interesting that Dottor Tibaldi didn't mention the death of Fortuna." Betta led Rick through the main gallery.

"But understandable. If it had been just the two of us, he might have brought it up, but not with you there." Rick looked around as they entered a new room. "Here's the Canova room; tell me about him."

Betta returned happily to her role of docent. After viewing the sculpture they spent a long time with the Jacopo works, walked through an archeology section, passed quickly through rooms reflecting the natural history interests of the museum's first benefactor, and then viewed paintings from the nineteenth century. Rick found once more that what Americans might consider very old art was considered modern in Italy. Every term is relative, especially in the art world. Betta checked her watch and told Rick that she had to get back to the gallery to help her father. As they walked toward the entrance they passed the door to the large room they had seen earlier, the one featuring the works of Jacopo da Bassano.

"Just a moment, Betta." On the single couch in the middle of the room a man in a rumpled suit stared at the painting before him. "It's Professor Gaddi. You remember which one he is. I should go over and talk to him."

"Of course, Riccardo." She gave him a kiss on the cheek. "Call me. *Ciao.*"

Rick watched her disappear around the end of the corridor before walking toward the professor. The old man's eyes never wavered from the picture before him, a colorful scene filled with figures gathering around Christ, who knelt on the pavement before the only woman in the grouping. Merging columns behind the figures gave the impression they were in a temple or other public building. In the distance, idyllic landscape added a Leonardesque touch.

"Professor, may I join you?"

Gaddi snapped out of his reverie. "Ah, Riccardo; of course, please do."

Rick took a seat and turned his attention to the painting. "I sense that this may be one of your favorite Jacopos in the collection. Am I right?"

He smiled at Rick before returning his eyes to the painting. "One of many favorites, it recounts the story of Christ and the adulteress. He is pestered by the scribes to make a pronouncement on the woman and her punishment, and his reply is that he who is without sin should cast the first stone. It is a memorable phrase, at the same time unfortunately a sad commentary on mankind."

"But a true one." He noted the contrast between the faces of the Philistine men who surrounded the adulteress and that of Christ.

Gaddi nodded in silent response. They continued to study the work until the old man spoke again. "It is always a pleasure to spend time with Jacopo, but I hope this investigation is ended soon. I must return home."

"Classes to teach."

Gaddi shook his head. "Classes are the least of my concerns. The students can wait, and usually would prefer to wait. No, Riccardo, my concern is more personal. My wife is ill, has been for several months, and I cannot leave her side for long. Our daughter is there now, but she should return to her own family."

"Is your wife receiving the medical care she needs?"

Gaddi kept his eyes trained on the canvas. "The doctors of the health service try their best, but she doesn't improve. I can't afford to take her to a private clinic or out of the country. Not on a professor's salary." He turned to Rick with a wry smile. "I didn't mean to burden you with an old man's problems, Riccardo, but there is something about you that makes me feel comfortable talking about it."

Rick didn't know how to respond. He could do nothing for the poor man, but if letting him talk about his problems had helped, he was glad to listen. There was one thing that Rick could do, which at least would get Professor Gaddi back to his home sooner—he could help solve the murder of Fortuna.

Rick found the police station easily. Ever since the time of the Red Brigades, heavy security had been added to *questure* around Italy, and bureaucratic inertia made it impossible to draw it down in more tranquil times. An armed and body-armored policeman, a bored look on his face, stood in front of the building, facing a triangular square below the castle which dominated the highest point on Bassano's hill. Perhaps in ancient times the work of keeping the peace had been lodged behind the castle walls. Now it simply moved outside them to make it less imposing for the average citizen. Once inside the station Rick realized he could be in any police station in the country—like going into a McDonald's and finding the same atmosphere, uniforms, and aromas. He walked to the desk where a bored sergeant sat reading a magazine with pictures, the pages barely visible below the counter.

"Riccardo Montoya to see Detective DiMaio. He may be expecting me." That wasn't true, but Rick didn't think DiMaio would mind, and it got the attention of the sergeant. He asked Rick to please wait, and disappeared through a door behind him. A few moments later DiMaio's face popped from a door of the waiting area, and he waved Rick toward him.

"Riccardo, I thought you might have skipped town. I was about to send your photo to the border guards." He slapped Rick on the back and led the way down a corridor into a windowless office that held a desk with one chair on either side, a metal filing cabinet, and a coat rack. "This room used to be a broom closet, but there wasn't enough room for the brooms. Please sit. What news? Have you discovered Fortuna's murderer?"

Rick sat in a metal chair that creaked slightly under his weight. "I came by to ask you the same thing. I've been trying to find out something about those two missing paintings."

The policeman nodded slowly. "I see. An interesting diversion while you wait for us to solve the homicide. It will be embarrassing if you find your paintings before we find the murderer."

"I assumed that you and Occasio would have had the culprit in shackles by now."

DiMaio shrugged. "Things don't move as quickly here as in Rome, which is quite ironic, really. No, we do not have even a strong suspect yet. Still sorting out the details." Rick leaned forward and waited, and the detective took the hint. "The place where the body was found has been thoroughly checked out—oh, but you don't know where poor Fortuna was found, do you? It was in a side street, an alley really, near the museum." He noticed Rick's reaction. "Which would put suspicion on someone from the museum, you're thinking. Not necessarily. It could be that the murderer wanted us to think that a museum employee was involved, or he wanted the death to be connected with the site of your little seminar."

"Or just coincidence."

DiMaio snapped his fingers and pointed one at Rick. "*Bravo.* So the murder scene is irrelevant. Especially since our forensic people think he was brought there from the place where he was, in fact, done in. Could have been anywhere." He glanced around the room and grinned at Rick. "Well, likely not here."

"So he was killed somewhere else and then dumped. From a car?"

"That is most likely. He was bleeding from a stab wound, and we unfortunately did not find a smeared trail of blood where he was dragged through the streets, leading us back to the site of the murder. That would have helped."

"Indeed."

DiMaio rubbed his chin. "We interviewed the waiters at the restaurant, and they confirmed what we'd heard from the others, including you. The way they remembered it—and we showed them a photo of the victim—Fortuna talked with everyone at the end when you were all standing around drinking grappa. One waiter said he recalled our victim spending a long time at the very end with two of them. He wanted everyone to leave so he could go home."

"Who were the two?"

"From the description it was Sarchetti, the art dealer from Milan, and he confirmed that when I talked to him this morning. The other was Tibaldi, of the museum."

"So they closed the place up."

"It appears so. Tibaldi stayed in the private dining room to thank the waiters, since he was the nominal host. The waiters confirmed that. And Sarchetti says he talked with Fortuna for a few minutes outside the restaurant before our victim went his way, which was not toward the hotel." He paused for effect and lowered his voice. "Off to his appointment with murder. *Un omicidio sfortunato*, you could say."

Rick was impressed by the play on words with Fortunato's name. "Very unfortunate indeed, for him."

"So true."

A harsh voice interrupted the conversation. "What's he doing here?"

Rick turned to see Inspector Occasio in the doorway, eyes squinted and mouth twisted into a frown. Both men got up from their chairs.

"I had some more questions for Signor Montoya, Inspector. I wanted to cross check his answers with what we've gotten from the other witnesses."

His expression unchanged, Occasio looked at Rick and then back at his detective. "Finish up with him. I have something for you to do." His short steps were audible after he left. DiMaio listened for a moment before turning to Rick.

"Probably needs coffee. But Riccardo, I have told you what is happening, now you must give me your thoughts. The nephew of Commissario Fontana must have something to tell me since he has taken the trouble to come my office. Or is this purely a social call?"

"I wish I could help, Alfredo. The mystery man here, as you told me yesterday, is Franco Sarchetti. He shows up at the conference as something of an interested non-academic, and now he is, by his own admission, the last person to see Fortuna alive."

DiMaio leaned forward, glanced at the door and back at Rick. "Perhaps you could nose around a bit, get to know Signor Sarchetti better. You being, of course—"

"Yes, I know, Alfredo, the nephew of Commissario Fontana."

"Exactly. But don't tell Inspector Occasio I suggested it."

After the darkness of DiMaio's office, Rick took a few moments to adjust his eyes to the sunshine in front of the police station. The small square had been filled with cars jammed every which way when he'd walked through it earlier, and it seemed even more congested now. He watched an old *cinquecento* as it tried to squeeze between two larger cars to claim enough space to be out of passing traffic. Even if the driver is able to do it, Rick wondered, how would the man get out of the car? Through the canvas sunroof?

He was awaiting the outcome of the car's maneuvers when something dark caught his eye. He looked up to see a dark blue sedan pull out of a space at the top of the square and disappear around the building on the corner. Could it be? Seeing the car made him realize he hadn't mentioned the night's incident to DiMaio. Just as well; it could have been some drunk teenager and the detective would think him paranoid. But if anything else happened…

The thought was interrupted by his cell phone, a local number he didn't recognize. "Montoya."

"Riccardo, this is Stefano Porcari."

Why would this guy be calling? "Signor Porcari, how are you?"

"*Bene, grazie.* I have been regretting my abruptness when we met yesterday in front of the hotel. Perhaps you could come by the bank for a coffee. I'd like to hear your impressions of the seminar, a neutral observer, so to speak. If I want to convince the board to sponsor such events in the future, I need to decide myself if they are worthwhile."

"It would be my pleasure."

"Good. Where are you now? I can send a car."

Rick kept the phone to his ear and looked around, spotting a sign on a corner wall. "I'm in Piazza Marconi."

"No need for a car. You're only a block away."

Chapter Eight

Everywhere in the world banks choose offices that project wealth and stability, solid structures that instill confidence for both investor and borrower. Italy added another factor. The very word "bank," after all, derived from *banca*, the table set out by early Florentine bankers on the streets of Rome, and Italy always prided itself on being the cradle of modern banking. So Italian financial institutions projected age and longevity as part of their image. By Italian standards the Bassano bank was not old, dating only from the mid 1800s, but the building was from an earlier period, creating an aura of sedate respectability. The front of the building didn't help to identify it as one of the usual styles found in Italian construction. The columns could be neoclassical or Palladian. Decoration around the windows looked out of place, perhaps added later when tastes changed. It was one of Rick's pet peeves, that a perfectly lovely medieval church had been ruined when another style was grafted onto it, especially when the change was Baroque. But he could not, by any means, be considered a serious architectural scholar.

Not helping to project the image of trust was the building's system of bulletproof doors, set up like an air lock, that Rick had to pass through to gain entrance. The main lobby's high ceiling, ornately decorated with gilt and allegorical paintings, drew his eye upward. As Rick took in the decorations, a younger man in a dark suit studied Rick with a rigid frown before stepping up.

"Signor Montoya?" The words were clipped, with a touch of impatience.

"Yes. To see Signor Porcari."

"I know that." He turned and began to walk away, but stopped and glanced back. Rick took the hint and followed him through a set of tall wooden doors to the inner offices of the bank. The man tapped on another massive door, opened it carefully, and stepped back to allow Rick to enter, all the while keeping his eyes averted.

Rick's thoughts, for some reason, reverted to Spanish: *muy simpatico*.

Porcari sat behind a wooden desk the size of the door Rick had just passed through, and equally polished. Holding his phone to his ear, he silently mouthed a word of welcome and waved Rick toward a configuration of soft leather chairs at one end of the room. And a large room it was. Crawling down the vaulted ceiling were a series of *groteschi*, those strange figures which had come into decorative popularity when unearthed on the walls of Nero's golden house in Rome. The walls of this room, however, were pure white, the better to show off a series of paintings, large and small, opposite the windows. Rick assumed that their placement was to keep them as far from natural light as possible, since each looked both old and valuable. He settled into one of the chairs and waited for Porcari to finish. The wait was about two minutes, after which the banker stood.

"Let me get us some coffee, Riccardo." He pressed a button on his desk, barked an order, and walked to the chair opposite Rick. "When I saw you in front of the hotel yesterday I was in a bit of a hurry. Didn't have time to thank you for what you did for the conference."

"It was my pleasure. I learned quite a bit myself."

The banker unbuttoned his jacket and folded one knee over the other. His black shoes were polished to a perfect sheen. "So you were not an expert on Jacopo before this week." He chuckled and turned up his smile. "I have always had an interest in art, but knew nothing about the man before I took this position. I made a point of studying him, and have become a great admirer. It is almost a requirement of residency in Bassano to be well versed on Jacopo. His life and work are taught in the schools here."

"Civic pride is always positive. And important to the bank, I would imagine."

"Indeed. And you have conveniently brought the conversation back to the bank's support for the seminar. I would be interested in your impressions of the program, Riccardo, since you are an outside observer. It was not a small sum that the bank spent on its sponsorship, and I must assess if the money was well spent."

Rick took a moment to gather his thoughts. "I assume that what interests the bank most is the effect your sponsorship had on its image within the city and the *provincia*, and I have no way to measure that. But as far as the seminar itself, in comparison with others I've worked, I would give its organization very high marks."

He was interrupted by the arrival of the coffee, brought on a tray by a secretary. The cups and saucers were local ceramic, as would be expected in a city which specialized in the craft. She placed the tray on the table between the two men and departed. Rick eased himself forward, somewhat difficult given the deep cushion, added some sugar to his cup, stirred it, and carefully settled back. His host did the same.

"Yes," said the banker, "my impression mirrors yours. Tibaldi did well. He seems to have an aptitude for organizing that would not be expected from a specialist in works of art."

Rick put down his now empty cup and looked up at the wall. "You have quite a collection here yourself, Dottore."

The banker was still stirring his cup. He looked at the walls as if noticing them for the first time. "Not mine, Riccardo. The bank has acquired a number of works over the years, some from estates in foreclosure, others in lieu of payments, and a number purchased as investments." A slight smile formed on his mouth. "There is no rule that says a bank must deal only in real estate, stocks, and bonds, in order to make a profit."

"And it makes for a very impressive office."

Rick expected that Porcari would at least mention the painters of some of the works, but instead he stared at his cup and took a first taste of the espresso. His face turned serious. "And this murder business, Riccardo. It hasn't helped the image of the bank, to use your phrase. I've been told that you've been helping the police. Are they close to solving the crime?"

He likes to get directly to the point, Rick thought. "I wouldn't say I'm helping the police, except that I translated when the inspector spoke with the foreign participants in the seminar. So I don't know if they are close or far from finding the murderer of Fortuna."

The banker studied Rick's face as if deciding the sincerity of his answer. "In my opinion the police should be looking at someone in the man's past. I only met him here at the seminar, but from his abrasive manner I would have to imagine that he had many enemies. One of them must have followed him here and killed him." He carefully placed his cup, still half full, on the tray next to Rick's.

"I'm sure Inspector Occasio is looking into that possibility."

"I certainly hope so." He did not try to disguise a glance at his wrist. "Riccardo, I have someone coming in a few minutes to ask for a rather sizable loan and I must prepare my answer."

Rick opted not to ask if the loan decision had already been made. Instead he thanked Porcari for the coffee and took his leave. Fortunately, Mr. Personality was nowhere to be found. As he walked down the marble steps of the building into the street, Rick tried to figure out, as any Italian would, the real reason the man had asked to see him. Asking Rick's opinion about the seminar was clearly only an excuse. Feeling him out about what he knew about the investigation? That was certainly part of it, though others had asked him about it, too, including the museum curator and even Beppo's uncle. Porcari also gave Rick his opinion on the case, hardly a brilliant theory, about a possible murderer. Was the man thinking Rick would report it back to the police? One thing was sure, the banker was not pleased that

Rick was not forthcoming, and someone so prominent in the community as Porcari would not be used to that.

He took a deep breath and turned a corner, his boots clicking on the stones of the street. On a bare wall, among funeral notices and movie advertising, he spotted a now-fading poster for the seminar. They'd been put up all around the city, but for the first time Rick stopped and read it. The art was a gaunt self-portrait of Jacopo da Bassano, under which ran the basic information about the event: dates, time, and place. Below that, in prominent lettering and logo, the Bank of Bassano got its due credit for sponsorship.

An aging Jacopo stared back at Rick, trying to decide what to think of this young person in strange boots and clothing. The artist wore the attire of his time: a dark skull cap and heavy coat with a long, fur collar which indicated status and perhaps wealth. The lines on his face and the graying beard spoke of a man who had labored all his days, but the expression said that such labor was a normal part of life. Rick wondered what Jacopo would have thought of his fame hundreds of years after this *ritratto* had been painted. Long overdue? He didn't look like a vain man; certainly not if this were a self-portrait, given the prominent wrinkles and other signs of aging. There was no pride in that face, only the look of a man ready to go back to work. A true artist.

As he studied the likeness, it occurred to Rick that something was shared by everyone he'd talked to in the previous twenty-four hours. Beppo's uncle, the museum curator, and now the banker—they all didn't just know art, they collected art. Franco Sarchetti was also in that group of collectors, the man on the suspect list of both Innocenti and Detective DiMaio. And of course there was the enigmatic Caterina Savona. What could be her game?

He tucked that thought back into his brain and continued his walk, reaching a corner with a street that ran along the top of a grassy slope. A low hedge and a sidewalk edged the top of the hill, the kind he would have rolled down as a kid. The windows of the houses on the opposite side of the street enjoyed what must have been the best view in the city. The green valley that began at the bottom of the hill continued, with minor undulations, until it reached the base of the mountains in the distance. Rick had been on this street during his morning runs but while puffing along hadn't given the vista its proper due. He stopped now to sit on one of the benches next to the hedge row and took it in. The street was silent except for the occasional car that came through the stone gate a few hundred feet ahead and drove past him. The bench caught shade from one of many trees, exactly alike, which ran along the top of the hill. Each had been lovingly trimmed to form an umbrella shape from the thick leaves. He walked to the thin trunk of the tree nearby and noticed that it held a small plaque with a black-and-white picture of a young man. He read the inscription, and found that the man, a partisan, was killed in reprisal by the Germans during the last days of the war. So that explained the name of the street, Viale dei Martiri. As Rick continued up the sidewalk toward the hotel he saw faces on each of the tree trunks and couldn't help wondering if Karl Muller had made this walk. If so, did he wonder if Grandfather Muller had been a part of these atrocities?

It was not Muller whom Rick ran into at the hotel, but Muller's British friend George Oglesby. Rick glanced through the doorway of the bar and saw him sitting alone staring at himself in the mirror, a half-filled glass of beer before him. Just before lunch was not a time of day when Italians drank beer, if there ever was such a time, so the Englishman had the place to himself. Even the bartender was nowhere to be seen. Oglesby's disheveled look was enhanced by a sweater that might have been woven from remnants of an old carpet. He glanced up and saw Rick's image between the glasses behind the bar.

"Rick. Come join me."

Rick took the place next to him. "Thanks, George. Where's your friend Muller?"

"Karl had an appointment. Seemed rather secretive about it, I dare say, and I didn't press him. Doubt if he's meeting some lady friend, but you never know. He does come down to Italy from time to time. He's a bit of a collector of things Italian, I know, but I'm not sure if that includes *signorine*."

Rick's ears perked up. "What does Muller collect?"

"Like so many of us, he dabbles in art. We really should spend our spare time with stamps or coins, rather than what we study all day long."

"Does Muller collect contemporary art?"

"Not sure. I think whatever catches his eye." He suddenly realized that there was no glass in front of Rick. "What are you drinking, my friend?"

"Nothing for me, thank you. And you would have to go around the bar to get it."

Oglesby laughed. "Marcello will stick his head out in a moment. He has a sixth sense about when my glass reaches a state of emptiness. So tell me, what have you been doing to pass the time while under house arrest?"

"Seeing a bit of the city. There wasn't the chance during the seminar."

"Helping the constabulary on the side, like you did for my interview?" He took a long pull on his beer.

"Not really, George. How have you been spending your time?"

He took a deep breath. "I have a dilemma, Rick. My wife is Italian, as you likely did not know, and her family lives not far from here. I had told her that I would not have time, with the program, to call on them this trip, as much as I would love to do so. And of course I wanted to fly to her side as soon at the seminar ended. Now with this damned murder investigation, I have been held here against my will."

"I sense, George, that you are not anxious to drop in on the in-laws."

The man sighed again, deeply. "You sense correctly, Rick. Lovely people, of course. And we do spend a week with them at Fossalunga every summer. But my Italian is rudimentary at best, good only for reading art history texts which, as I'm certain you know, bear no resemblance whatsoever to colloquial speech. When we are with her parents, Anna chatters away with her mother, leaving me to fend for myself with the old man. To say that he and I don't have much in common, including a workable mutual language, would be a gross understatement. The thought of spending time with the Vizentin family by myself is daunting."

"But they must feed you well."

Oglesby groaned. "Alas, that is another problem. Anna's mother is a cook without peer. And you know the two choices Italian mothers offer when they place a dish in front of you."

"*O mangi, o ti butto dalla finestra.*"

"Precisely. And since I don't want to be thrown out the window, I eat. And eat. And when my mouth is full I know that I don't have to talk. Rick, the last time we spent a week there I returned home a stone heavier."

A face poked out from a door behind the bar. Oglesby gave him a thumbs-up and Rick wagged a finger to indicate he didn't need anything. The bartender walked over, took the now empty beer glass, and put it in the metal sink next to a stack of coffee cups. Then he lifted a clean glass from the shelf and filled it by pulling down a tall plastic knob behind the bar.

"*Ecco,*" said the bartender.

"*Grazie*, Marcello," the Englishman answered before turning to Rick. "If you promise not to tell my mates back home, I'll confess that beer served cold can be quite satisfying. I believe this one is a local brew, but I'm not sure." He took a long swig. "So tell me, Rick, how long do you think it will take the local coppers to solve this murder?"

"I've always heard that if they aren't solved in the first few days, the chances of doing so at all drop radically. So I assume that's the case here."

"They can't keep us here forever."

"There are worse places to be cooped up."

Oglesby looked at his glass. "I suppose you're right."

◇◇◇

When Rick walked out of the bar into the lobby he nearly collided with Erica, grabbing her to keep from knocking her down.

"Sorry about that, *cara*. I was escaping from an Englishman who doesn't want to visit his Italian *suoceri*."

"Don't they feed him well?" She straightened her skirt, though it didn't need it.

"Why am I not surprised at your question? Anyway, it's very complicated. Where's Jeff?"

"He's getting the desk clerk to make a table reservation at a place that's been recommended nearby. Why don't you join us?"

"I'd really love to, but—"

"Rick!" Jeffrey Randolph's voice called from across the lobby as he strode toward them. He shook Rick's hand and then took Erica's. "You're keeping busy, I trust, under the circumstances?"

"I'm trying."

"I just asked Ricky to join us for lunch, but he has another engagement."

Randolph reluctantly took his eyes from his fiancée and turned to Rick. "That's unfortunate." He looked quickly around the room and said in a lowered voice: "You could have given us the lowdown on the investigation. After all, you are helping the police, and Erica tells me that your uncle is a high muckamuck in the Rome police."

Rick stole a look at Erica to see if her English had progressed enough to know the meaning of "muckamuck," but her expression showed nothing. "I'm just as much in the dark about it all as you, Jeff."

"I, for one, think the murder is somehow related to the seminar." Randolph's voice remained conspiratorial. "And even, mind you, connected to the two missing Jacopos."

Erica asked the question before Rick could. "What makes you think that, Jeffrey?"

"There was a very heated exchange the final day between Fortuna and Paolo Tibaldi, the museum curator, about the missing paintings. I had the distinct impression, listening to your translation, Rick, that there was more to it than just an academic difference of opinion."

"Jeff, do you think Tibaldi could be responsible for Fortuna's death?"

The professor blinked, realizing what he'd said. "I probably wouldn't go that far. But there was definitely friction. Perhaps you couldn't see their expressions from inside your translation booth. Or see the faces of the other participants. Every one of them was glaring at Fortuna, clearly agreeing with Tibaldi."

Rick changed the subject slightly to put Randolph at ease. "What is your opinion about the missing paintings? Do you think they'll turn up?"

The reply was not what Rick expected.

"I do. And I don't think we'll have to wait another sixty years. Something is going on, otherwise we would not have seen these dust-ups. The art history community is like an extended family, and we exchange e-mails and letters frequently. There's been a lot of comment about this."

It sounded to Rick like chatter in terrorist cells, but he didn't voice the thought. Could this be the "rumblings" that Beppo had mentioned? He looked up and found his excuse to take leave of the couple. "There's the person I was going to meet. I hope you have a nice lunch." He waved goodbyes and hurried to a man standing at the reception desk. When the man saw Rick he smiled, thanked the desk clerk and walked to meet Rick. He wore the same drab suit but with a striped shirt and brown tie.

"*Salve*, Riccardo, how are you?"

"*Bene, grazie.* Were you looking for me, Signor Innocenti?"

"I was. Something has come up that I must tell you about."

"Is Betta all right?" It came out without Rick thinking. The old man smiled.

"Yes, yes, she's fine. Though I worry about her riding her brother's motorcycle." They walked to a group of chairs at one side of the lobby but when they reached them, the older man stopped. "Have you had lunch, Riccardo? There is a small place around the corner that makes excellent *tramezzini*. Unless you'd like something more elegant."

"That sounds perfect."

Rick pushed the door of the lobby to let Innocenti step to the sidewalk. In the time Rick had been inside the hotel a thick cloud had pushed across the sky from the west, bringing with it a drop in the temperature and a few gusts of wind. They walked to a small bar a block away where a knot of teenagers, unfazed by the chill, sat at their sidewalk tables eating their sandwiches, sipping soft drinks from cans, and chattering. The two men squeezed past them, entered the bar, and walked to the glass counter behind which sandwiches of varied fillings were neatly stacked between moist napkins. Rick chose tuna with pieces of green olives, Innocenti the sliced hard-boiled egg and lettuce, and each asked for a glass of white wine. The man behind the counter went to work: *tramezzini* were carefully removed from the stack with wood tongs, placed on small plates over paper napkins, and passed across to the two customers. Plates and glasses in hand, they walked to a round table in one corner and sat. After they tapped wineglasses and exchanged the appropriate meal wishes, Innocenti got down to business.

"What I wanted to tell you has to do with our little investigation. Unofficial investigation, I should add. I had an unusual visitor to the gallery this morning, Professor Gaddi from the seminar. I hadn't met him during that program—you'll remember I sat in the back. Not sure how he found the shop, but perhaps he's visiting various art galleries."

Rick finished his first bite of the *tramezzino*. "It's as good a way to spend one's time as anything else, when you can't leave town. Especially if you have an interest in art."

"Perhaps. He began by commenting on the exhibit we have on the walls at the moment; a local artist, you'll remember. But then he began asking about older works of art, if we ever sold paintings of old masters from the Veneto. He was curious about how it all worked, if such items come on the market often, that sort of thing."

"Did he ask specifically about buying or selling?"

"Neither, or both, depending on how you might take his words. He never came out and said he wanted to buy or sell anything. It was all very curious."

"It sounds like Professor Gaddi could be suspicious of something, just as we are, and has taken it upon himself to investigate."

Innocenti sipped his wine. "A second unofficial investigation? But he could have heard something about the missing paintings, and as a serious scholar of Jacopo, he would want to find those two missing works as much as anyone. Who knows, he may be a chapter short of the definitive book on the artist and needs them to finish it."

"Or he could be bored and is walking around Bassano. Perhaps I should keep an eye on the man."

Innocenti finished his sandwich. He'd been hungry. "Already taken care of. Elizabetta is following him right now. I would have asked you but you would be easily recognized. Unless you have some training in tailing people."

Rick thought about the question. His uncle had talked about surveillance many times, which Rick had found fascinating. "No. Has Betta?"

"She's done it a few times."

"A woman of many talents, your daughter."

Innocenti nodded. "What about Sarchetti? He's still the mystery man here, Riccardo. Have you had a chance to talk to him?"

First DiMaio, now Innocenti, wanting him to cozy up to Sarchetti. He pulled out his phone and dialed the hotel. "Let's see if I can track him down." The operator put him through to Sarchetti's room, but Rick was not optimistic he'd find him there.

"You're late calling."

Rick was taken aback by Sarchetti's greeting. "Signor Sarchetti? This is Riccardo Montoya."

The man on the phone laughed. "Ah, Riccardo. Excuse me, I was expecting another call. Thanks for not hanging up. What can I do for you?"

"Well, I'm always looking for feedback on my work, and since we are all stuck here for the time being, I've been asking everyone if the translation worked well for them." He grimaced at Innocenti, who smiled back.

"I thought your translation was excellent, Riccardo, but let's get together and chat about the conference in general. I'd like to hear what you thought of it. And it would be good to talk to someone who isn't a stuffy art professor."

"When would be convenient, Signor Sarchetti?"

"Riccardo, I'm not much older than you, so I'm Franco. I have appointments this afternoon and a dinner engagement. How about after dinner? A grappa at that famous bar at the end of the bridge at say, ten o'clock?"

Rick held up a thumb, and Innocenti returned the gesture. "*Va bene.* I'll see you then, Franco." He clicked his phone off. "That was easy."

"I could hear some of what he was saying, and got the impression he wanted to talk."

"Let's hope so." They both looked up when they heard the bang of the barman emptying the coffee grounds from the espresso machine. "A coffee, Signor Innocenti? Perhaps a piece of pastry to go with it? Those *tramezzini* were small."

The older man stroked his chin. "To clear the palate. I noticed a *crostata* next to the cookies, perhaps a slice of that."

Rick rose to his feet. "I noticed it, too." He walked to the counter, put in the order, and came back to his chair. "He'll bring it." Innocenti nodded and smiled as Rick settled into his seat. "Signor Innocenti, if you don't mind me asking, how did you get into this business with helping the art police?"

Innocenti sighed. "It was many years ago, when my wife was still alive, bless her." His eyes focused on something outside the window, which Rick suspected was the image of Signora Innocenti. "It was a simple case, really. A man showed up at the gallery with some artwork to sell. It was by an artist who, by coincidence, I knew well, even to the extent that I was aware of who owned which of his canvases. To make a long story short, he was arrested and I came to the attention of the culture police."

"And Captain Scuderi?"

The barman appeared with a tray and placed the espressos and desserts on the table, along with a bowl of sugar. The *crostata* had the usual thin-edged pastry base covered by a yellow custard and decorated with sliced fruit: kiwi, strawberry, and grapes. The triangular slices on their plates were colorful works of art, but not colorful enough not to eat. They both added sugar to their coffee and picked up forks. After a bite, Innocenti answered Rick's question.

"That was well before Captain Scuderi joined the office."

Rick assumed it was also before Beppo had arrived at the ministry and begun his swift rise through the art police bureaucracy.

"It was quite small then," Innocenti continued, "but as you know it has grown considerably. The press always finds out quickly when a major work of art is recovered due to their efforts, and that doesn't hurt their efforts to grow their budget."

They finished the desserts, picking up the errant crumbs with the tines of their forks, and sipped the last drops of coffee.

"It has been a pleasure, Riccardo. And I will be anxious to hear about your encounter with our Signor Sarchetti at the bridge." He slipped on his overcoat and they walked out to the sidewalk. The outdoor tables and chairs stood empty under the gray sky, a chill wind weaving its way through their metal legs. The two men started back toward the hotel, pulling their coats around their necks. Rick looked up to see Caterina Savona coming toward them, wearing a long wool coat and boots, her uncovered head bent against the cold wind. As she got close she noticed him and stopped.

"Riccardo, we meet again. And again in passing." She pulled a hand out of her coat pocket and pushed back the hair from her face. "Perhaps it is time we actually sit down and talk. Though I can't now."

"Fate seems to be telling us that, doesn't she?" Rick replied before tending to his manners. "Caterina, I'd like you to meet

Signor Fabio Innocenti, Betta's father. Signor Innocenti, this is Caterina Savona, also a recent visitor to Bassano, with whom we had the pleasure to dine at Signor Rinaldi's villa."

As the two shook hands a strange look spread over the face of the older man as he murmured a greeting.

"Signor Innocenti, it is my pleasure." She turned to Rick. "I'm afraid I'm late to a meeting, but we really should meet other than to say hello, Riccardo."

"Absolutely." They watched her continue down the sidewalk away from the hotel entrance. "An interesting woman," Rick said. "At least I think so, not really knowing her." He looked at Innocenti's puzzled expression. "Had you met her before, Signor Innocenti? She did not seem to have recognized you."

"No, no. I've never seen her before. There's just something…" He shook his head quickly before turning to Rick. "I must get back to the gallery. With Elizabetta out I had to put up the closed sign, and now there are probably dozens of clients milling around the door, anxious to buy paintings." He shook Rick's hand. "My pleasure seeing you again, Riccardo."

He crossed the street and hurried in the direction of the gallery while Rick stood on the sidewalk watching. One thing was sure—Betta had not told her father about being forced off the road the previous night. That would be expected—she didn't want him to worry. What Rick found strange, however, was the man's reaction to meeting Caterina. The enigmatic Signora Savona now became even more mysterious.

Chapter Nine

Italian fashion, like fashion everywhere, swung on a long pendulum. What was *di moda* one year would inevitably fade, replaced by something else which held its place for a few years before something new appeared or, just as likely, the previous fashion returned. Cynics would say that the industry rather than the consumer drove the fashion, and they would be correct. Nowhere was the pendulum more evident than in men's ties. As Rick studied a long rack of them, he was grateful that in Italian tie fashion, traditional had regained its proper place. It was a mere few years ago that every man in Italy was wearing ties that looked like they'd been copied from the canvas of an abstract impressionist. Now the selection, thankfully, included stripes and sedate prints. Since he was picking out something for Uncle Piero, traditional was a requirement. He finally settled on a tie with stripes of various widths and colors, pulled it off the dowel holding the display, and walked to the cash register. His cell phone rang as he handed over his credit card, and he smiled when he read the number.

"*Ciao, Betta, dové sei?*"

Her voice was so low he could hardly hear her. "I'm here at the ceramics museum, watching Professor Gaddi. I was starting to think that following him was a waste of time, but he just got a phone call and seemed to get quite agitated. Now he's looking at the exhibits, but his mind isn't on it. He keeps checking his watch."

Rick pushed the phone to his ear while he signed the slip. "It sounds like he's going to meet someone. I'm close by, I'll come over there but stay out of sight."

"All right, but—wait, he just looked at his watch again and now is walking toward the exit. I'll talk to you later." She was gone.

Rick turned off his phone, took the small bag from the sales-girl, and asked her the location of the ceramics museum. As he'd thought, it was only a few blocks away. He thanked her and left the store, folding the bag carefully and slipping it into his coat pocket. A few minutes later he reached the street he wanted, narrow and one way, on a hill sloping down toward the river. He could see what he assumed was the museum entrance in the distance, a wide gate in the high stone wall guarding what had once been a patrician residence. He kept close to the stores on the opposite side of the street, ready to duck in if Gaddi materialized. Instead he saw Betta appear at the gate, an annoyed look on her face. She was surrounded by a gaggle of children, all dressed in the same school uniform. Rick strode quickly down the hill. When he reached her the kids were all talking at once.

"The old man? He was picked up by blue Fiat."

"No, it was a Simca, and it was gray."

"Dark green."

"Purple. It's my favorite color."

"Lady, are you a cop?"

"Is the old man a criminal?"

"Did he rob a bank?"

Betta was about to attempt an answer when a nun appeared, glared at Betta and Rick, and shooed the brood away. They giggled and chattered as they were led down the street.

"That's the problem with eyewitnesses," Rick said. "They're never reliable." He was grinning but Betta was not.

"I waited for a few moments so I would not be right on his back, but when I got out he was gone. All we can be sure of, it appears, is that he got into someone's car."

"I hope it was red, that's my favorite color."

She poked him. "Now what do we do?"

"I don't think there's much we can do about Gaddi, and it's now late afternoon. Why don't we do some research? We may find out more about the paintings that way than from following these people."

"I know the perfect place to do it."

Rick was hoping that the perfect place for research was at the computer in Betta's apartment, but it turned out to be the city archives. They were housed in a seventeenth-century stone building which, along with a baroque church, took up one side of a wide piazza. The structure had once housed a religious school for the wealthy male youth of the city, connected not just structurally, but also spiritually and administratively with the adjacent church. In the last century, when the school closed, its building had been taken over by the municipal government and everyone agreed that the school library was the perfect space for the archives. Two stories high and domed by a multicolored skylight, wood bookshelves ran along its walls, the top volumes reached by a rolling ladder. Circling the room was a balcony with more shelves, some of them encased in glass. Grouped on the floor below, desks with gooseneck lamps allowed the scholars to pore over their work, though today they were armed with computers rather than quilled pens and parchment. To make things easier, the entire center of Bassano, including the archives, was a WiFi hot spot.

"Impressive, isn't it?" Betta spoke in almost a whisper, in keeping with the atmosphere.

"It certainly is. Are all those books real, or are they painted on?"

"You can go check while I see if Gisa is here." She went off in search of a friend who was the assistant director of the archive. Rick walked to the shelves and couldn't resist pushing the tall ladder that was attached with rollers to rails at both top and bottom. A man looked up from his book when it squeaked, flashing an annoyed grimace. Rick ignored the man and checked out the books, which were indeed real—hand-tooled leather spines embossed with gold leaf titles. He recognized none of them. Betta appeared at the door with an attractive woman her same age, dressed in jeans and a baggy sweater. Reading glasses with leashes were her only concession to the librarian stereotype. Betta introduced her and they shook hands.

"Gisa says they have files on the final days of the war, so there could be something in them about the missing paintings. There is also an archive on Jacopo da Bassano that could be useful."

"I'll bring out what we have, Riccardo, and if you don't find what you need I can try somewhere else." Gisa waved her hand at one of the tables. "Why don't you two sit here and make yourselves comfortable." She gave Betta a wink and walked off.

"What was that about?" Rick asked.

"She'll be calling me tonight to find out all about you."

"But you don't know all about me."

"What little I do know she'll pry out of me."

About half the places at the tables were occupied. Rick noticed that the age of the researchers fell into two groups: quite young or quite old. The gray heads were salted among the youth who were either university students or the upper class from the *liceo*. The younger *studiosi* were evenly divided by sex, while the older ones were mostly men. Another indication of changes going on in Italy.

Gisa appeared after a few minutes, her arms filled with files which she placed on the table between them. "*Buona lettura.*"

She left, and Rick and Betta started to go through the materials, she taking those dealing with Jacopo, he the war history.

Mixed among lists of names and dates were stories of the final months of the war. Rome had been liberated in June of 1944, after which the Allies continued their slog up the Italian peninsula, but Bassano remained under German control until the following spring. The stories told of a city in chaos, withering under the iron hand of the occupying power with dreadful consequences for those who resisted. But the Italians had eventually won their city back. Since he knew history was written mostly by the winners, Rick could not help wondering how much of these accounts was accurate. And as importantly, what stories had remained untold and never reached the archives. After a half hour he found something and tapped Betta on the arm.

"Here's something interesting." He ran his finger down a page of names and stopped at one. "A German infantry battalion, stationed east of here before finally withdrawing into Austria, had an *oberlutnant* named Karl Muller. That's the name of the German participant in the seminar, and he told me that his grandfather had been in this area during the war. Do you think that he was named after his grandfather? The ages would be about right."

Betta leaned back in the chair, removed her glasses, and rubbed her eyes. "I'm not an expert in German names, Riccardo, but I think both Karl and Muller are quite common."

"You're probably right. Have you found anything in your Jacopo materials?

"The two paintings went missing in April of 1945, which we knew already."

"That's about the time Lieutenant Muller was here in the province."

"Along with thousands of other armed men and women. But you'll like something else I found—the villa from which they were taken is just east of here, near Fossalunga."

"Don't tell me."

She held up her hand. "I don't think it's where we had dinner, but it's possible. The names of these villas change when someone buys them, as you'd expect, unless the original owner was famous enough that it adds prestige to the new owners and they keep the old name." She realized that her voice had gone back to normal, and looked around to see if anyone was listening. No one was. "But there are quite a few villas around this province," she whispered. "There is a folder of clippings from the time about the paintings. The family didn't have them insured, not that they would have been covered anyway."

"War and insurrection. Standard disclaimers in insurance policies."

"There was some talk that the family had sold them before the war when they were in trouble financially, but didn't want to admit it. Then they claimed the paintings had been stolen to save face. But that could be some journalist inventing a good story. The family denied it."

"I'd be shocked if that really happened."

Betta frowned. "That they'd sold the paintings?"

"No, that an Italian journalist would invent a story." He put his hand over hers. "I think we've done enough research. Unfortunately I have to check my e-mails at the hotel. I'm expecting a contract from America to do an Italian version of a magazine article. It's morning in America, and that's when people back there usually send me messages. It is the weary lot of a professional translator, always waiting for the next job. But I will be done by dinner time."

"I should go back to the gallery."

"While you're working, think about where I'll be taking you for dinner."

◇◇◇

As Rick started up the Viale dei Martiri gathering clouds began blocking out the view of the mountains, perhaps in anticipation of a late afternoon shower. He had brought a raincoat on the trip, but his umbrella sat in the closet of his apartment in Rome. It had been wishful thinking, assuming the weather would be perfect. Now he might have to buy one. His phone rang, a local number.

"Montoya."

"Riccardo, this is Alfredo."

"I forgot that you had my number, Detective."

"We are the police, we know everything. I need to talk to you, and it would be better not on the phone."

"That sounds serious."

"Not really. I just don't want anyone walking by the broom closet and listening to what I'm saying."

"Do you want me to come to the station? I'm close."

"No, not here, Occasio is prowling. Why don't we meet at the castle? Have you seen our wonderful castle yet?"

Rick turned and looked toward the highest point in the city where an ancient stone tower rose stiffly from the surrounding buildings. "I can see it from here."

"I'll be at the gate in two minutes."

Rick hung up, turning in the opposite direction from the hotel. He reached the piazza and walked up a narrow street to the castle entrance where DiMaio stood, looking at his watch. "You're late."

"I stopped for a coffee."

They passed through a set of heavy wooden doors into a courtyard. Ahead was the *duomo*, the city's oldest church and a sanctuary in former times of danger when the thick, high walls of the castle gave welcome protection to the people of Bassano. Another massive structure, likely the barracks, was built out from another part of the wall. Rick looked up and saw that the sky was still clear. "What did you want to tell me?"

They walked together on the stones, the heels of Rick's boots tapping softly. A group of tourists stood near the entrance to the *duomo*, but otherwise the courtyard was deserted. "Inspector Occasio is finding it peculiar that you have been poking around the city, talking with people."

"Is he having me followed?"

DiMaio studied the pavement as he walked. "If he were, he likely wouldn't tell me. No, he found out in another way. The inspector always makes a point of cultivating the pillars of the community, and apparently Dottor Porcari mentioned that you'd been to see him at the bank."

"Porcari neglected to mention that it was he who invited me to stop in."

A wispy cloud came into view over the high wall. "That detail did not reach me, and I don't know if it got to my *capo*. Have you been seeing other names on our suspect list?"

"Of those few people I know in Bassano, almost all are on your suspect list, Alfredo. And you'll remember I've been look-ing into those lost paintings, so the people from the seminar are the logical ones to talk to about them." Rick tried to keep the annoyed tone from his voice, but was unsuccessful. "Is that all you wanted to ask me?"

"Well, that, and if you've had any contact with Sarchetti."

"I called him, and we're meeting for a grappa tonight at the bridge."

DiMaio stopped and slapped Rick on the back. "Excellent, I will look forward to hearing what he has to say. Your uncle would be proud of you. Don't let Nardini's grappa cloud your mind." He looked up at the darkening sky. "And speaking of clouds, it appears that we are going to have a shower. I would love to continue our chat, but I should let you return to the shelter of your hotel. There was something else I wanted to ask you, but it can wait until you call me this evening. You'll call me immediately after seeing Sarchetti, will you not, Riccardo?"

"You'll be the first to know of our conversation."

The tourists had noticed the clouds and were hurrying out of the gate ahead of the two men. When Rick and DiMaio parted ways at the edge of the piazza, the first fat drops hit the pavement.

Rain had fallen hard on the tile roofs of the city, spilling out of drain pipes into the stone streets where it gushed downward, eventually finding its way to a river already swollen from the storms upstream. The afternoon shoppers took their time indoors or waited under the protection of the covered walkways for the deluge to stop, as they knew it would. After an hour the sky brightened and the last light of the afternoon led people to their homes. Rick had missed most of the meteorological excitement, safely tucked in his hotel room, bent over his laptop.

Now he and Betta faced each other at a table in a room crowded with diners. The storm brought a cold front behind it, but inside the restaurant the atmosphere was anything but chilly. Betta looked fetching, wearing a slightly brighter shade of lipstick that accented her green eyes and dark hair. Her white silk blouse was opened just enough to show a pearl pendant dangling from a gold chain. There were no rings on her fingers, and her nail polish was clear. The same perfume Rick had gotten to know so well on the back of the motorcycle drifted toward him across the table. Again he tried to identify it, and again he failed.

"Gisa called me, as I knew she would. I couldn't tell her much but promised I would learn more this evening." Betta picked up her wineglass and eyed Rick over the rim as she drank. It was a cue, if Rick had ever seen one, and he took it.

"Not a whole lot to tell. My father was an exchange student in Bologna where he met my mother. He went into the diplomatic service and managed to be assigned to Rome, which is where I spent my early years. We did some tours in South America and came back to Rome where I went to high school. Then on to the University of New Mexico, following in my father's academic footsteps. Studied languages, most of which I already knew thanks to where I'd lived, and then started working life as a professional translator. Decided to move the business to Rome. It is doing well, bringing me to remarkable places like Bassano del Grappa where I meet beautiful and exotic women." He picked up his glass, tilted it at Betta, and drank.

"No, uh, women in your life, at the moment?" She showed a perfect row of white teeth. "It's not important to me, but Gisa will ask."

"Not before yesterday. Will that satisfy Gisa?"

"I'll let you know tomorrow."

Rick tilted his head and gazed deeply into green eyes. "And you, Betta, any men in your life at the moment? Present company excluded."

The light in her face dimmed for an instant and then returned. "Not at the moment, Riccardo. I did, but it didn't work out."

He reached across the table, placing his hand over hers. "I'm sorry to hear that. I hope it was for the best."

Betta took a breath and forced a smile. "It was. Sometimes you think you know someone and then suddenly you find that they're very, very different."

Rick didn't want to know the details. "Well I, for one, am very happy that you've moved on." He picked up the menu on his plate. "So what do you recommend for a first course? All I had for lunch today with your father was a *tramezzino*, so it has to be substantial."

"*Polenta e salsiccia*, it's very good here. But you may not have room for anything else."

He closed his menu. "It's the chance I'll have to take."

Betta decided on the *zuppa pavese*, and after taking their order the waiter refilled their glasses from the carafe of house white, a smooth Soave. Rick purposely steered the conversation to more trivial things—TV personalities, the latest movies, and the inevitable subject anywhere in Italy, the differences between living in Rome and elsewhere. No politics, and certainly nothing about the murder or the lost paintings.

Her first course arrived in a wide bowl, a crusty piece of rustic bread topped by an egg floating in a the hearty broth that had cooked it. The waiter enhanced the dish with spoonfuls of grated cheese. Rick's golden-yellow polenta spread over most of his plate, topped with two links of thick sausage.

"You may be right, Betta, this is clearly not the child's portion."

She laughed and asked Rick about going to college in America. He told her a few stories, but confined them to some tame anecdotes about professors and classes. Perhaps when he knew her better he would get into the seedier side of Albuquerque. He'd prided himself in being at home in both biker bars and lecture halls. She recounted her years at the University of Padova, commuting from Bassano while working part time in the gallery. They concluded that despite the contrasting geography and languages of the respective colleges, there were as many similarities as differences. When their *primi* were finished, Betta brought the conversation back to business, such as it was.

"Riccardo, my father told me you're meeting with Sarchetti tonight. It sounds very mysterious. What do you hope to get from him?"

He shrugged. "Don't know, really. I'll ask him about the paintings. I'm sure he'll bring up Fortuna's murder. He sounded interested in talking, so perhaps he's got something to say. Or wants information from me."

After the waiter removed their dishes, she spoke. "Tell me what you did this morning after I left you at the museum."

Menus appeared again for them to order the second course, and Rick studied his. "I talked with Professor Gaddi there in the museum. The man is in some difficulty due to the illness of his wife, but he acted fatalistic about it. His behavior in the afternoon didn't seem in character with that, but we don't know what he was up to when he rushed out of the ceramics museum. It could end up being completely innocent. Then I talked with the detective about the murder case. They're not making much progress. He asked me to find out what I could from Sarchetti, so he too will be anxious to hear if anything comes from this meeting tonight."

"Does he suspect Sarchetti in the murder?" Concern spread over her face.

Rick wondered if he'd said too much, and decided it would be better not to mention Inspector Occasio's annoyance with his meetings around the city. "They suspect no one and everyone. I think it's normal to go back and talk with everyone involved more than once. That would include me." She didn't appear satisfied with the answer so he chose to avoid the subject of the murder. "Then I got a call from Porcari and he invited me to have a coffee at his office at the bank."

"You went to the bank?"

"Quite a building, I was impressed." He noticed her face and stopped. "Betta, what's the matter?"

She picked up the menu. "Nothing really, Riccardo. Only... well, the relationship I mentioned that didn't work out? He's an employee at the bank. You wouldn't have met him."

Rick ordered spinach warmed in butter for his second course, claiming that, as she warned, the polenta had filled him up.

After walking Betta to her apartment, Rick stopped in the middle of the piazza and looked upward. A quarter moon lit the night sky despite a row of round clouds that marched one by one in front of it. The stone pavement glistened under his boots, wet from the shower, and puddles forced him to zigzag before reaching the protected sidewalk on the other side. He had time before meeting Sarchetti, which he needed to sort his thoughts. Was he the only one who saw a connection between the missing paintings and the murder? DiMaio certainly did not, and if it had crossed Betta's or her father's mind, they didn't let on. There was no firm evidence linking the two cases, only the victim's expertise and Rick's hunch. *Intuizione* was the word in Italian that came into his interpreter's head, but the translation didn't do "hunch" justice. What could emerge that would join the two cases? He tried to focus on the facts and block out the distractions, like Erica's surprise return, poor Gaddi's financial problems, and now this guy he'd seen in the bank who had to be Betta's former flame. No, worry about the right stuff, like whether Beppo's uncle was involved in shady dealings, or what the Savona woman had to do with anything. The ideas bounced around in his brain, but after walking a few blocks they finally came to rest with a conclusion. Better to put your efforts into the mystery of the missing paintings for the moment and hope for some break in the murder case.

He turned onto the Via Campo Marzio, reminding him that Bassano was, nominally at least, founded by the Romans. The Campo Marzio in Rome, the Field of Mars, was the area where the soldiers were quartered and trained. No doubt the legions needed somewhere to march in Bassano, so it must have been nearby. The street sloped downward toward the river, changing its name on the way, and passed the ceramics museum where Gaddi had vanished earlier in the day. The street was joined by two others at the eastern end of the bridge. Two buildings on the sides of the entrance were in fact one, joined at the upper floor to form an arch for pedestrians to pass under and onto the bridge. On the left was the entrance to the Grapperia Nardini that, according to a plaque outside, was founded in 1779.

The interior looked like it still used the original furnishings. The wood of the bar and rustic tables shone under decades of varnish and wax, its dark hue covered in one spot by a crude painting of a man drinking grappa. There were enough bottles of grappa lined up on the shelves behind the bar to supply the French and Austrian armies, which the place claimed to have done in the nineteenth century. Above the bottles, almost touching the wood-beamed ceiling, a row of small copper vats stood at attention. Every surface—wood, glass, and copper—was polished to brilliance, as were the marble tiles on the floor.

Three men sat on benches at a table in the corner, hunched over their tiny glasses, their ages difficult to decipher. Their creased faces and rough hands could have been the result of a long life or a shorter one involving hard work. Their dress was no help, wool jackets and pants, tie-less shirts. Likely pensioners, Rick concluded. Pensioners were everywhere in Italy.

Sarchetti stood at the bar watching the barman pour a dram of grappa into a crystal glass. He turned when he heard cowboy boots on the marble. From his rheumy eyes, unbuttoned collar, and loosened tie, Rick surmised that this was not the first alcohol the man had consumed this evening.

"I would not have started without you, Riccardo." They shook hands. "Guido here tells me that we should try this one; it has the flavor of almonds." He picked up the glass and studied the clear liquid. "Like arsenic."

Rick was not a fan of grappa—to him it all tasted like something better used to heat one's house—so he ordered a thick, dark *digestivo*. He was served and they tapped their glasses.

Sarchetti displayed mock disappointment at Rick's choice. "Grappa is one of the great inventions of man, Riccardo, prevalent in the northern climes, of course. It is a drink to be taken with reverence." He took a taste. "And this place claims to be the oldest distillery in Italy. We are standing on sacred ground."

Rick sipped his amaro, its herbs spreading over his tongue and down his throat. "You seem in a good mood, Franco. If I can call you Franco."

"I am in a good mood even if you can't call me Franco, but please do." He raised his glass again. "Yes, coming here this week proved to be a trip well worth making, though I had my doubts. Who would have thought that a town like Bassano would yield such results for an art dealer like me?"

"Buying or selling?"

Sarchetti smiled. "Nothing firm yet. Since many of my clients prefer anonymity, I would not reveal transactions, in any case. But I've also made what I hope will be some excellent contacts for future business."

"Caterina Savona among them?"

There was a chuckle and he took another sip of his grappa. "So you have met Caterina. You do get around." He drained his glass. "Are you sure you won't try some of this? It's smoother than I expected." When Rick declined, Sarchetti gestured to the barman to fill his glass. "This business with Fortuna. What do you make of it?"

Rick expected the question. "I'm just as puzzled as you must be. The man was not universally loved, for certain, but who would detest him enough to do him in? It doesn't seem possible that it was someone from the seminar—these academics don't seem capable of such things."

"Not all the suspects are academics. I'm not, for example, nor are you. Nor is Porcari, the banker. And Tibaldi from the museum is more of a bureaucrat than an academic, though he wouldn't agree with my definition." He lowered his voice. "It's a mixed group, Riccardo. There could be a murderer among us. And university professors have been known to kill." The barman had gone over to the table and said something to the old men, who emitted a collective groan. "Is is possible that the place is closing? Well, he can't throw us out yet." He held tight to the tiny glass with sausage fingers. "And what are the police telling you? You must have developed a little rapport with them, doing the translations."

"Inspector Occasio is not the type to share his thoughts. It was he who questioned you, Franco, wasn't it?"

"It was. At the end I was trying to decide who was more *antipatico*, the policeman or the murder victim. I had some dealings with Fortuna recently, and the two must have gone to the same charm school."

"Dealings?"

Sarchetti waved his hands as if trying to erase his comment. "Nothing of any consequence. I have contact with art specialists frequently, even ones like Fortuna. You are sure you won't have another shot?"

Rick had another sip, but was careful not to drain his glass. "No, I'm fine. Franco, I was curious what you thought of those exchanges in the seminar about the two missing Jacopo paintings. Do you think they'll ever be recovered?"

Sarchetti did not answer at first. Instead he stared with bleary eyes at Rick, as if sizing him up, a half smile on his lips. "Riccardo, my friend, I don't think we'll ever see those paintings. That said, there's no one who would be happier to see them than I—assuming I could get a piece of the action, of course. But such transactions are often done under great secrecy, with both seller and buyer dealing only with a middle man, never even meeting each other. So if it happens, or if it has already happened, it may never become public."

"Have you ever brokered that kind of secret sale?"

"If I told you I had, it would no longer be a secret, would it?" He threw down what was left in his glass and set it roughly on the bar. "I should not have another, though I'm sure I could persuade Guido to give it to me. Our chat has been a perfect end to a very pleasant day for me, Riccardo. If the police continue to be unsuccessful in finding Fortuna's murderer, and they keep us in Bassano, we will have to do it again. But next time you will have to try the grappa."

Rick reached for his wallet. "Shall we walk back to the hotel together?"

"Keep your money in your pocket, Riccardo. It is my pleasure." He tossed euro notes on the bar and waved off any change. "You go on back. I think I will take in some fresh air and watch the river from the bridge for a few minutes before I return."

◇◇◇

Rick climbed the hill slowly and tried to remember everything that Sarchetti had said. Like any good Italian, the man had chosen his words carefully, revealing what he wanted and keeping the rest a mystery. But the grappa, on top of what must have been an ample amount of wine, had helped loosen the man's lips. He had been anxious to brag about unspecified deals, and Rick was ready to listen. What Sarchetti did not realize was that Rick knew of his visit to the villa of Angelo Rinaldi. It would make sense that any sale he'd made in the last few days was with Beppo's uncle, a serious art collector. But could it have been Caterina Savona? Rick looked up and realized that without thinking he'd walked into the piazza of the Innocenti gallery and apartments. He looked up at Betta's window and saw a faint light. He put his hand on the cell phone in his pocket, but left it where it was and continued through the square, returning to his thoughts about the meeting with Sarchetti. DiMaio will be disappointed, he thought, since most of the conversation had been about the missing paintings or other subjects, like grappa, not connected with the murder. Sarchetti had mentioned unspecified dealings with the murder victim, but that must have come out when Occasio questioned the man. No, most intriguing was his mention of doing business in the little town of Bassano, of all places.

He walked through the second piazza and started up the long, rectangular square that ran next to the church and the entrance to the museum. A young couple strolled slowly and aimlessly along in the general direction of the river, holding hands and deep in quiet conversation. Ahead, an old man, hunched over, leaned on his cane as he crossed the square and disappeared down a side street. Rick thought about calling DiMaio, but what little he had to tell him could wait until the morning. He tightened the belt around his coat and wondered if the city was in for another storm. He wasn't familiar with weather patterns in this part of Italy but assumed that, like everywhere, they moved from west to east. Perhaps here they blew down from the mountains or up from the Po Valley.

Rick entered the hotel lobby and walked toward the reception desk when he heard a familiar voice.

"Rick, come join us." In one corner of the room, near the entrance to the bar, sat Jeffrey Randolph and Erica, half-filled glasses of wine on the table between them. Reluctantly Rick detoured and moved to them as Randolph rose to greet him. "We were enjoying a nightcap after a fine meal. Why don't you join us?" Erica's smile signaled agreement.

"Thank you, but nothing for me. Where did you have dinner?" It was the most natural of questions in Italy.

"The restaurant where you had your final banquet," answered Erica as Rick took a seat across from them. "It was very good. I had a chance to try the famous local asparagus."

"But they aren't quite in season, dear. The waiter warned you."

"I know, Jeffrey, I know. They were still very good."

Hmm. "I've heard about the white asparagus festival they do here every year," Rick said. "I noticed a poster for it on the street."

"We will have to come back for that sometime, won't we Erica?"

She frowned, but mercifully, Rick's phone sounded before she formed an answer. Who would be calling at this hour? Perhaps it was Betta. He excused himself, walked to a corner of the lobby, and pulled out the phone. A local number that looked familiar.

"Montoya."

"Riccardo, you were going to call me after your meeting with Franco Sarchetti." There was an edge of annoyance in Detective DiMaio's voice which came through the background noise.

"It's late, Alfredo. I was going to wait until morning. And how do you know that I'm not still talking with the man and you're interrupting us?"

"For one thing, I'm here with him on the bridge."

Now it was Rick's turn to show annoyance. "You could have waited to interrogate him until I told you how our meeting went."

"I may be a fairly competent policeman, Riccardo, but even I can't interrogate a dead man."

Chapter Ten

"It was kind of you to send a patrol car to get me, Alfredo." Rick hoped the sarcasm in his voice was noticeable.

Red and blue lights from the police vehicles bounced off the buildings around the entrance to the bridge where Rick and DiMaio stood. About halfway across the span, inside a circle of police, cameras flashed like welding torches, lighting up the underside of the roof with bursts of white. Despite the activity on the bridge, the only sound came from the engine of the crime scene truck whose wires spread out along the pavement. The men on the bridge went about their work in silence. Occasio stood back from the group around the body, his arms crossed, a scowl on his face.

"Inspector Occasio wanted you brought here in handcuffs when he heard you were the last person to see Sarchetti alive. I convinced him that a car was sufficient."

"I was not the last to see Sarchetti alive, Alfredo."

"Of course. A slip of the tongue. I trust you are ready to answer some questions?"

Occasio had spotted Rick and was walking toward them with quick, short steps. As he walked, he gestured roughly to a man standing near the entrance to the bar. The man came toward them and Rick recognized him as the one who had served him his amaro earlier in the evening. He wore a coat over his white shirt and black tie, and he was shivering.

Occasio jerked a thumb toward Rick. "Is this the one who was with the dead man this evening?"

The barman looked at Rick. "Yes, Inspector, he—"

"That's all I need." Occasio turned to Rick. "Now, *Mister* Montoya, you will tell us what happened when you and Sarchetti left the bar?"

Rick looked down at the inspector, glad he wore cowboy boots that added even more inches to his height advantage. A voice inside him, possibly Uncle Piero's, told him to stay calm and not say anything foolish, despite the antipathy toward the man. "I can only tell you what I did when I left, Inspector, since Sarchetti was still inside. He told me that he wanted to spend a few moments looking down at the river from the bridge, so I departed while he was finishing his grappa and climbed the hill to the hotel. He said he needed some fresh air, which I took to mean he wanted to clear his head after the alcohol."

Occasio's eyes narrowed. "You expect me to believe that you just left him? Staying at the same hotel, it would make sense to walk back together. Tell me what really happened."

"I just did, Inspector. Perhaps Sarchetti was going to meet someone on the bridge and didn't want to tell me." He was rubbing his palms on his hips, something he always found himself doing—almost unconsciously—before a fight. The intimidating talk was the guy's modus operandi, but Rick was damned if he'd let it work on him.

"His meeting was only with you, Montoya. And just why were you having this little encounter?"

Rick glanced at DiMaio. "Since we haven't been able to leave Bassano, on your orders, I've become interested in the story of two missing paintings by Jacopo Bassano. I wanted to ask Sarchetti about them."

"And everyone else in town? You've been up to something, Montoya, and I intend to find out what it is." To DiMaio he said: "I'll finish up with the crime scene crew and we'll leave immediately to see Signor Rinaldi." He turned and walked quickly back to where two men in white jumpsuits were examining the body.

Rick hoped DiMaio was watching his boss and didn't notice the look on his face when Beppo's uncle was mentioned. "Where is it that you're going?"

DiMaio was deep in thought, but snapped out of it. "What? Oh, we got an anonymous call today about Sarchetti having met with a man named Angelo Rinaldi. It was what I was going to tell you this afternoon when it started to rain. It didn't seem urgent at the time, but we didn't know then that Sarchetti was going to get murdered, did we? So my *capo* and I are going to drive out to question the man."

"It's almost midnight."

"We called ahead. Occasio is always deferential to prominent citizens, such as the banker Porcari, and it seems that Rinaldi is quite an important businessman."

"I know, Alfredo, I had dinner at his villa last night."

DiMaio's eyes widened, and then a smile spread over his face. "My, my. The inspector is correct, Riccardo, you have indeed been getting around. And why would you be dining with someone who is now part of a murder investigation?"

"Rinaldi's nephew is a good friend from Rome. He called his uncle to tell him I was in Bassano and the man invited me for dinner. If I'd known he would be involved with the police I might have found an excuse to decline the invitation."

Occasio separated himself from the crime scene and walked quickly toward the waiting police vehicle. He directed a scowl at Rick and the detective.

"I have to go," said DiMaio. "We'll talk tomorrow. Try to stay out of trouble."

Rick watched them get into the car, wishing he could be a fly on the wall when they interviewed Beppo's uncle.

With the hotel sitting at a high point just north of the city, there was no way for Rick to avoid a steep return climb at the end of his pre-breakfast run. After that first morning in Bassano he settled on a route that provided a good mix of grass and ancient stone, beginning with a drop down to a large park below the

Viale dei Martiri. Besides offering natural surroundings to look at, the horizontal terrain allowed his muscles to warm up slowly in preparation for the rest of the run. By the time he finished weaving his way along the flat path he was ready to take on some inclines. Then he would climb up through the town and down to the bridge, crossing the river before turning back again to make the final ascent to the hotel. It was a *percorso* he would miss when he returned to the flat streets of Rome. But the advantages of early morning jogs near his apartment were many. Thanks to the maze of streets, the combinations of routes were endless, and nothing compared to a run through Piazza Navona just as the sun was coming up. But he'd already decided that on his first morning back in Rome he'd run down to the Tiber, cross it at Castel Sant' Angelo, go up Via della Conciliazione, and take a turn around St. Peter's Square before retracing the route back to his apartment.

This morning, after the required stretching outside the hotel, he crossed at the traffic light and started down the street that led down to the park. As in so many ancient Italian towns, parking inside the walls was problematical if not illegal for non-residents. But unlike many other towns, Bassano had found space at the bottom of the hill for a large *parcheggio* to accommodate commuters and tourists. There were hundreds of spaces, and even at this hour they were beginning to fill up. A moment after passing the parking lot he was jogging along a path that wound its way through grass and trees. No doubt on any sunny Sunday afternoon the wide field would be filled with families enjoying the green, open space. At this early hour on a weekday, Rick was the only one on the path which formed a large figure eight extending from one end of the park to the other. He breathed in the smell of recently mown grass made more fragrant by the rain that fell the previous day and still sparkled among the blades.

At a bend in the path, amid the green grass, he found himself looking up at a bulky metal figure, and today he decided to stop. On top of a stage of weathered marble stood a dark bronze statue of a soldier staring off into the distance. He gripped his rifle in one hand and held out the other as if presenting an invisible offering in its palm. A helmet protected his head, and a long cape was frozen in place by some long-ago wind. The inscription on the stone read simply: *AI RAGAZZI DEL '99.*

Rick had read about "the boys of '99" who had the misfortune of coming of age in 1917, the year Italy entered the First World War. They had been conscripted by the tens of thousands, suffering and dying in the snowy trenches and mountain passes of northern Italy. The face on this *ragazzo* did not look like that of an eighteen-year-old, but combat and fatigue would have taken its toll, even on a boy, so it may well have been an accurate portrayal. Rick took a breath and started off again. Across the open grass was the return section of the path, which he would reach after running a large loop through more grass and trees. In the distance he saw a lone female figure jogging back toward the city. She was dressed in black tights and sweatshirt, a matching sweat band around her forehead keeping her dark hair from her eyes. Only her running shoes, a dark red, kept the outfit from being one color. Rick smiled, trotted across the expanse of field, and waited for her to approach. Only when she was a few yards away did she notice him.

"Riccardo." Caterina Savona stopped and took in a few breaths. "Are you a runner too?"

"It's the best way to start the day."

"I have a rule never to interrupt my morning run, but I'll break it for you." Her hands were on her hips and she breathed heavily. "They told me this morning at the desk that we have another murder."

"I know. The police talked with me last night since I had a drink with Sarchetti just before it happened."

She looked hard at him. "Oh dear, that doesn't sound good. But you're not in jail so they must not consider you a suspect."

Rick shrugged.

"Do you think it could be connected to the other death?" She was still breathing heavily. "What was his name?"

"Fortuna. It would be too much of a coincidence if it didn't." He considered adding that it might be connected with the two missing paintings, but kept it to himself. "Did Sarchetti say anything to you when you met him yesterday morning that might shed some light on why he was killed?"

She started jumping lightly on her toes. "No, we just chatted briefly. We were going to have dinner back in Milan. Riccardo, I'm starting to tighten up, so I must get back to my run. Let's talk sometime." She laughed. "I say that every time we run into each other." She waved and headed down the path toward the town.

Rick started to walk back to the other section of path, but turned to watch her. She had a good long stride, like someone who had been coached, and she kept her head down in concentration. Ahead of her a row of tall pines lined the path, forming a corridor of evergreen. He watched the morning sun reflecting off their needles when another glint caught his eye.

"Caterina!" he shouted. "Stop!"

Her head jerked back toward him, and she lost her balance, landing on her hip and leg. She skidded along the wet pavement and spun around to face him. The scowl on her face could have been for her own clumsiness or annoyance at Rick, who was now running up to her. "What was that for, Riccardo?" She rubbed her side while holding up a hand so he could bring her to her feet. But before pulling her up he pointed above her head.

"The sunlight picked it up from where I was standing. It was at just the right angle or would have been invisible."

A thin piece of wire strung across the path at about neck height. Rick brought Caterina to her feet and then walked to the tree where one end of the wire was wrapped around the trunk. He unwound it and carried it to the other side, leaving it on the ground. "That could have done some damage."

She rubbed her hip and stared at the wire on the ground. "I had my eyes on the path. That could have taken my head off. Who would do such a thing?"

"The police may have a theory."

Her head turned quickly toward Rick. "Police? No, I don't want to get involved with the police, Riccardo. It's just some horrible prankster. A twisted kid. No, we'll just keep this between ourselves." She came up to Rick and embraced him before turning back to the wire. "You may have saved my life, Riccardo. I owe you a big favor. But no police. This will be between the two of us." She continued down the path, but slower, and keeping her head up, as she disappeared around a bend.

Rick crossed the grass and returned to where he'd stopped running, determined to finish his normal route. There was no doubt in his mind that the wire was meant for him, and he knew why. Last night's murderer knew about the meeting on the bridge, and could even have watched from the shadows as Rick came out of the bar. If Sarchetti was killed because of something he knew, the killer could believe that Rick had been given that information. So Rick could be next on the list. But like Caterina, he didn't want to get the police involved. The last thing he needed at this point was a police inquisition or body guard.

The path started its loop before turning in the direction of the town. Though it was doubtful there could be another wire, he carefully scanned the trees when they came close to the path. Passing where Caterina had slipped, he thought about her reaction to the incident. She clearly wanted to avoid contact with the police at all costs. What was she afraid of? Should he ask his uncle to run a check on Caterina Savona? No, he immediately rejected the idea. It would mean telling him about the two murders, and that Inspector Occasio headed the investigation. He didn't want that. He would find out about Uncle Piero and Occasio in due time, after he got back to Rome. He puffed up the hill and into the town. The stone buildings and narrow streets of Bassano closed in on him, making him feel safer.

Rick sat in the hotel lobby checking his phone messages, his hair still damp from the shower. He was relieved—given their agreement to keep nothing important from each other when they talked—that there were none from Uncle Piero. There was one message to call from Betta, which must have come through when he was on his run. The girl gets up early, another plus. He hit the button for a return call.

"Ciao Betta, sorry I missed your call. I was on my morning run."

"I hoped it was that, and you hadn't been murdered."

What was it in her voice? Annoyance? Fear? "So you heard about Sarchetti."

"On the radio. It must be connected with the two missing paintings."

She certainly goes right to the heart of things. "I agree. But how?"

"I was hoping you'd figured that out. Have the police talked to you?"

"Last night. Let's meet so I can tell you about it."

"I was going to suggest the same thing. How about a bike ride to clear our minds? It always helps me. I'll pick you up."

He immediately remembered having his arms around her waist. "Sounds good. But I have work to do here. Detective DiMaio wants me to translate when they interview Muller and Oglesby again. They're in with—wait, Gaddi's coming out now." Rick watched a haggard Professor Gaddi emerge from the make-shift interview room. He gave Rick a weak smile and walked to the elevator. "The poor guy looks terrible. I'll call you when I'm done—it shouldn't take more than an hour."

"Fine, I'll await your call. Ciao." She hung up.

As Rick slipped his phone into his pocket Occasio appeared at the door followed closely by DiMaio. The inspector spotted Rick and turned to his assistant. He gestured toward Rick and spoke into DiMaio's ear before hurrying toward the door. A moment later the sound of a police siren wailed to life on the street outside and then disappeared in the distance. Occasio has left the building, Rick said to himself before walking to the detective's side.

"I don't get the pleasure of assisting the inspector in his investigation?"

DiMaio cracked a half smile. He looked tired. "Surprisingly he has left the interview of the German and the Englishman to me. I don't think he enjoys sharing the stage with a translator. Cramps his style."

"I'm starting to wonder if his style is to let you do all the work."

"I reserve comment on your comment." The elevator door opened at the other side of the lobby and George Oglesby appeared. "Before we talk to the Englishman, perhaps you would like to hear about our visit with Rinaldi last night after we left the bridge."

"I'm all ears." Rick signaled to Oglesby that they would be with him shortly, and the two men entered the conference room. The hotel had provided fresh water and clean glasses, but otherwise it looked the same. They took seats opposite each other.

"Angelo Rinaldi greeted us wearing a smoking jacket. I'd thought people only wore them in old movies, the ones where they used white telephones. And he wasn't even smoking. Occasio, as I'd expected, demonstrated the proper amount of obsequiousness with the man. No bowing and scraping, but close to it. Rinaldi waved it off—I almost think he was enjoying it all—and offered total cooperation, even after he was told that Sarchetti had been murdered. Not the reaction of a man who had anything to hide."

Rick shifted in the chair, remembering that at dinner Beppo's uncle never mentioned meeting Sarchetti. Of course he never said he hadn't, either. "What did he say about his encounter with the murder victim?"

"Strictly business, if you can call the sale of art a business. Sarchetti had been recommended to him by another business-man who is also an art collector, so he called Rinaldi when he got to Bassano."

"Did Rinaldi buy anything?"

DiMaio looked at his watch, as if remembering that Oglesby was waiting. "He said the encounter was simply to meet the man, to size him up. No offers made nor accepted. I suppose one has to be careful when one buys expensive paintings, and those on the walls of that villa looked very expensive."

You don't know the half of it, Rick thought. "Did he have an alibi?"

DiMaio chuckled. "It was almost painful for the inspector to ask, given the high status of Rinaldi, but he reluctantly did, and our host said he'd been at the villa alone all evening. Listening to opera, no doubt, in his smoking jacket. But his staff could corroborate his story if the inspector wished to interrogate them. Occasio waved it off. A pillar of the business community would be believed."

"It doesn't sound like you got much."

"No. Except that Occasio was able to make a new contact." He flipped open his notebook. "Let me move on to information that is actually verifiable and not the testimony of a peripheral suspect." He noticed Rick's frown. "Forgive me, Riccardo, but despite Rinaldi's being the uncle of your friend, we must consider him a suspect." He turned the pages of the notebook until he found the one he was searching for. "The initial medical examiner's report came in, which you may find of interest. Sarchetti was stabbed at close range, but since few stabbings take place at long range, no surprise there. The weapon was a knife, again expected. But it is almost certain that it was the same weapon that killed Fortuna."

"So the same killer."

"Riccardo, your powers of deduction are extraordinary. Your uncle would be proud."

Rick accepted the gibe, but could not help wondering why DiMaio was giving him such details of the investigation. A family connection with the police was one thing, but the detective was sharing more than would be expected under the circumstances. Certainly Occasio would not have approved.

DiMaio stood. "We should not keep our two foreign guests waiting, but let me mention one more thing. I talked to our colleagues in Milan this morning about Sarchetti. He apparently had some shady dealings, but nothing they could ever prove.

Exporting things he perhaps shouldn't have, that sort of thing. It sounded more in the purview of the fiscal police or even the art cops. They were going to check around to see if any Milanese criminal element could have had it out for the man. My guess is that they'll never come up with anything. Shall we talk to our British friend?"

When Oglesby entered the room Rick was not sure if he was wearing the same clothes as he had the previous day in the bar. Maybe he'd packed just enough clothing for the length of the seminar. And having the hotel do laundry is not cheap, especially if you need it done quickly. "You remember the drill, George, I'll translate back and forth for both of you."

Oglesby nodded deliberately, making Rick wonder if he'd already been to the bar. Ironically it was Marcello, the barman, who could confirm that the Englishman had not left the hotel all evening, since that question would likely come up. It did. DiMaio asked about other contacts with Sarchetti, and the answer was that there were none. Other questions followed, but the interview went nowhere, the policeman realized it, and grew impatient. Finally he thanked Oglesby for his cooperation, signaling an end to the session.

"Can I leave now? I mean return to England?"

"I'm afraid not yet," was DiMaio's answer, then duly translated. Rick was sure that Oglesby would be heading straight to the bar when he left the interview. When he was gone, DiMaio stared at his meager notes and gave Rick a silent wave of his hand to bring in Muller.

The German was dressed in a herringbone tweed jacket and brown slacks, a solid gray knit tie covering the front of his button-down shirt. Apparently in the fatherland one dressed well when meeting with the authorities, especially the police. He entered the room with a frown, but his mouth turned more pleasant when he realized that Inspector Occasio was not in attendance. They took their places, Rick sitting at the head of the table with the other two on either side to facilitate the translation. The detective was about to begin when Muller spoke.

"I should tell you immediately that I had dinner with Franco Sarchetti last night."

"Tell me about it," said DiMaio after Rick had translated. He turned the page in his notebook.

"He suggested that we dine together, saying that we're both prisoners in the town and should make the most of it. He also wanted to know if I was familiar with some art dealer in Munich he was considering doing business with. His German, by the way, is—or I should say was—quite good. He learned it in Vienna, and spoke with a definite Austrian accent. Do you speak any German, Rick?"

"Just enough to order a beer."

Muller nodded, and glanced at DiMaio. "Anyway, Sarchetti insisted that the dinner would be on him. Naturally, I accepted." He took a sip of water and continued. "The man was in a jocular mood, which surprised me, since he had been somewhat serious on the few occasions during the seminar when we'd spoken. With the help of the wine, he dominated the conversation. The food was excellent, so I made a point of enjoying it and let him talk. He began by giving me his opinions of everyone at the seminar, and they were so negative I wondered what he would have said about me outside my presence. Fortuna was a bully, George Oglesby is a lightweight, the banker Porcari is pompous—that sort of thing. I almost defended my friend George but decided he was too far into his cups to make a difference."

Rick translated, marveling at Muller's English fluency by using the phrase "in his cups." DiMaio scribbled a few notes, but mostly listened.

"He asked about the dealer in Munich, but I think it was perfunctory. What he really wanted to talk about was the two missing Jacopo Bassano paintings." The policeman looked up quickly at Rick before writing something down. "Have you heard about this mystery, Detective?" When DiMaio indicated that he was familiar with the two paintings, Muller continued. "Sarchetti wanted my opinion on whether they would ever be seen again. The issue had been hashed over in the seminar, goodness knows, but for some reason he wanted to hear from me directly. I told him." He paused to take another drink of water, but also, it appeared, for effect. "They will never be seen again, at least in our lifetimes. The works of a second tier painter are not immediately recognized by the layman, and I believe they are hanging on the wall of someone who has no idea of their value. A Leonardo, or a Titian, people know that style, but who is aware of how Jacopo Bassano painted? Or even who he was? Very few."

"And how did he react when you told him?" It was Rick who asked, but DiMaio didn't seem to mind, likely because he knew of Rick's interest in the subject.

"I expected him to be disappointed, but he wasn't. I remember that he merely smiled and poured himself more wine. By then we were into our second bottle. Then he brought up the murder of poor Fortuna. I expected that, of course, since it is the reason we have all been forced…the reason we have all remained in Bassano."

"Did he have any theories?" DiMaio's voice indicated he didn't expect much in return for his question.

"He was convinced, Detective, that it was one of us involved with the seminar. I trust you've been told of the argument between Fortuna and Tibaldi, the museum curator. There may have been other confrontations outside the formal part of the program. Fortuna had a way of antagonizing people, if I might understate."

"We've heard that a lot," said DiMaio. "Did Sarchetti tell you that he was going to see anyone later in the evening?" His eyes turned to Rick, but Muller likely thought it was an invitation to translate.

"He did, but he didn't say who he was going to meet. When he asked for the check I recall him looking at his watch. I think it was about nine-thirty at that point. Yes, that would be about right, since I left him in front of the restaurant and walked back to the hotel. When I got there it was a few minutes until ten."

DiMaio tapped his pen on the table top. "Is there anything else Sarchetti said that could be helpful? Anything that sent up a red flag in your mind, especially now in light of what happened to him?"

Muller rubbed his chin in thought. "There was one thing, though it's likely of no consequence. When he was talking about Fortuna's death, he said something like, 'Well, that's one less Jacopo scholar to worry about.' He laughed when he said it, but I felt uncomfortable since I consider myself a Jacopo scholar. A very peculiar comment."

After Muller left the room, the policeman flipped through his notes before looking over at Rick. "What does the nephew of Commissario Fontana think of what our German said?"

"It sounds like Sarchetti was already in a good mood during his dinner and it continued when I met him on the bridge. He told me that Bassano had been good to him, though he wasn't specific. Perhaps some real business was transacted with Rinaldi, despite what the man told you and Occasio last night."

"Or Sarchetti thought there was a good chance of future business," DiMaio said, still reading his notes. "And that final comment, about one less Jacopo scholar?"

Rick shook his head. "No clue. Perhaps he'd had his fill of academics in this seminar. Can't say I blame him. But that reminds me of something Sarchetti told me at the bridge. He said in the past he'd had some dealings, whatever that means, with Fortuna."

"The man was an art dealer, perhaps he'd asked Fortuna to authenticate some paintings."

"That would make sense." Rick thought a moment. "What I found most fascinating in what Muller said was the exchange about the missing Jacopos. And Sarchetti's reaction when Muller told him they'll likely never be seen again."

DiMaio shut his notebook and tucked his pen into his jacket pocket. "There is one major problem with Muller's recollection of his meal with Sarchetti. I might add, Riccardo, that your uncle would have been the first one to point it out, and perhaps he did in the course I took from him. It's this: when someone describes a conversation with a murder victim, we can't consult with the dead man to get his recollection of the conversation, can we?"

"So Muller could have made it all up, to suit his ends."

"Precisely."

Chapter Eleven

The motorcycle had no problem with the steep curves. Rick swung his head to catch the views while he clung tightly to Betta's waist and joined with her body leaning left and right through the turns. They had ridden slowly through the town of Marostica, a few minutes west of Bassano and famous for its annual human chess match in the main square. That piazza was devoid of chessmen today, live or otherwise, but a few locals meandered across it, enjoying the rays of mid-morning sun. Betta left the narrow streets and climbed the road that ran along the side of the town. They drove outside Marostica's wall system, which looked from a distance like a short version of the Great Wall, complete with periodic bastions protecting it from invaders from above. At the top the *Castello Superiore* presided over the valley below with views over to Bassano on the east and, on a clear day, to Vicenza in the south. The castle was their destination.

Betta drove slowly through a gate in the wall to emerge in an open courtyard below the castle building. In classic Italian fashion the castle was now a restaurant, complete with tables outside, though at this hour the few set for lunch were still unoccupied. It was questionable that they would be used, since clouds began to form, blocking out the diagonal rays of sun and dropping the temperature. Instead, the diners at midday would likely be eating inside, in what Rick supposed would be a dining room fit for a king, or at least a duke. Betta brought the bike to a stop, lowered the kickstand, dismounted, and pulled off her helmet. She pushed her hand through her black hair, though it was so short nothing needed to be put back in place. Rick brushed his hair as best he could with his fingers, realizing that, for the first time in his life he was dating a girl whose hair was shorter than his. Dating? Is that what's going on here?

Carrying their helmets, they climbed a short set of stairs to the covered patio. Both wore appropriate attire for a motorcycle ride—blue jeans, short jackets, and boots. Except for the footwear, Betta's attire clung much more snugly to her body. Her boots were brown leather with the right length heel for the bike, with a strap peeking out from under the cuffs of her jeans. He wore the more casual of the two pairs of cowboy boots he'd brought on the trip. When they reached the top of the stairs Betta turned and made a sweeping gesture with her free hand.

"Do you have views like this in New Mexico, Riccardo?"

"Sorry to disappoint, but yes, we do. Did you know that, by square kilometers, you could fit all of Italy into the borders of New Mexico? In a state that large you can find a lot of different terrain, including views like this."

"Did you work for the state chamber of commerce?"

"It's a nice place, Betta, you should visit sometime." He found himself again looking into those green eyes and added quickly, "Can we get some coffee here, or is it too early? A cappuccino would be perfect to warm us up after the ride."

"I know the manager, I'll go in and ask." She put her helmet on one of the chairs and pushed through the door to the inside. Rick placed his helmet next to hers and sat down to absorb a view which was indeed spectacular. Areas of open fields and groves of trees spread out to the south, broken by an occasional small town or a strip of road. To the east and west the first wrinkles of the mountains started their climb to the Austrian border. Betta reappeared and took a chair across from him.

"*Due cappuccini* coming up." She leaned back and they both stared into the distance. Their silence was broken by the waiter's arrival with two large coffee cups. He took them off his tray and placed them on the table along with a bowl of sugar and a small plate of cookies.

"With Livio's compliments." The man gestured toward the plate. "Baked this morning."

"*Grazie*," said Rick and Betta simultaneously.

"You must come here often." Rick dropped sugar into his coffee.

"Not that often. But I spent a lot of time here last year planning for the wedding reception. The one that never took place."

Rick wasn't sure what to say, but sensed she wanted to talk about it. "With the guy from the bank?"

She took a sip and flicked the foam from her upper lip with her tongue. "Yes. We called it off about a month before the date. We were at a party with friends and he had too much to drink. There was an argument and he got rough with me, which was the wrong thing to do with my brother Marco there. I thought Marco was going to kill him, it took several friends to restrain him. By the end of the evening the engagement had ended." She stirred her coffee. "That's all there is to tell."

"I will remember what you said about Marco and be on my best behavior if I ever meet him."

She smiled. "My brother's a sweetheart. And I hope you will meet him."

"I do, too."

She reached across the table and covered his hand. Her fingers were warm from holding the cup. "Let's talk about something more pleasant, like murder and stolen art."

"If we must," answered Rick. He reached the cookies, using his free hand. "Unfortunately they appear to be connected. We now have one less person who could know something about the missing Jacopos, and he was our prime suspect. Maybe we've been deluding ourselves about the two paintings. Muller, the German professor, said again this morning that he thought they'd never be seen again." He didn't mention that it was during a police interrogation that Muller said it.

"Let's get to the paintings later. Tell me about last night."

He told her, leaving nothing out. "The inspector probably would have interrogated me longer if they didn't have to go talk to Angelo Rinaldi. It's very curious that they received an anonymous tip about his having met with Sarchetti at the villa." He looked carefully at her but she picked that moment to take and taste one of the cookies.

"Yes, very curious. These cookies are quite good, don't you think?"

Rick smiled and shook his head. "They certainly are. Speaking of villas, did we ever find out if Rinaldi's villa is the same one as where the paintings disappeared?"

Betta brushed a cookie crumb from her jacket. "It wasn't. The villa of the Jacopos was in Fossalunga, but Angelo's villa…"

"Fossalunga? Wait a minute. Remember when I told you about meeting with Oglesby, the Englishman, in the bar at the hotel?"

"Of course. Complaining about his *suocera* feeding him too well. You'd never hear that from an Italian."

"Right, likely not. But when you mentioned Fossalunga it came to me that it was the town where his in-laws live. Do you think…?"

She picked up another cookie. "I think we're grasping at straws, Riccardo. It would be perfect if they'd had the paintings, gave them to their English son-in-law, and now he's selling them to the highest bidder. But I doubt it. Coincidence. Just like it's coincidence that Muller's grandfather was around here in the war. But we can check it if you'd like. What was the name of his wife's family?"

He looked at the last cookie and then at Betta. She nodded, and he took it. "Let me think. It was a northern name, Venetian. You know, no vowel at the end." After a bite of the cookie he remembered. "Vizentin, that's it."

Betta patted her lips with the paper napkin and held up her finger before pulling out her cell phone. She scrolled through her directory and tapped on a number. "Ciao, Gisa. We're coming by to do some more research." She listened and rolled her eyes. "Riccardo is right here, Gisa, and might have heard that. Listen, could you pull out something about the town of Fossalunga? And any genealogical material on the Vizentin family that lives there? Separate it and we'll go through it when we get there. Right, Vizentin. We're in Marostica, so we should be there in about twenty minutes." Another pause. "Very funny, Gisa." She tapped the phone off and slipped it back into an internal pocket. "It's time to go back to work, Riccardo."

He held a hand over his heart. "It doesn't feel like work when I'm with you, Signorina."

"There you go again."

◇◇◇

Betta managed to squeeze the motorcycle into the middle of a row of Vespas a few meters from the entrance to the archives. Rick could almost feel the mini-bikes cowering in the intimidating presence of the Ducati. Carrying their helmets, they mounted the stone steps of the building and walked down a long hallway toward the reading room. An exhibit of crayon drawings mounted on panels set away from the walls lined one side, each identified by name, age, and school, on a card below.

"Future artists for your gallery," Rick noted.

"You never know."

"I remember the library in Albuquerque doing exhibits like this. It must be a requirement to get your international library license." There was no reaction from Betta. "There's actually no such thing as an international—"

"I know, Riccardo. There she is."

Gisa stood in front of a bulletin board outside the tall doors leading into the reading room. Today she wore another loose sweater with a long, knit skirt and burgundy clogs. She spotted them and walked in their direction.

"So good to see you again, Riccardo." The words were like honey, and spoken as if she and Rick shared some kind of secret. Her grin added to the impression.

"The pleasure is completely mine, Gisa. You are very kind to help us with our little research project."

The librarian held up her hands in defense. "What would you expect for an old friend?" She glanced at Betta and back at Rick. "As well as the new friend of an old friend."

"Okay, Gisa, that's enough."

"I was just starting to enjoy this," Rick protested. "But I suppose we have some work to do."

Gisa shrugged and looked them over. "I have the material in my office, and since I don't want our archive patrons frightened by the appearance of two biker gang members, you'd better read it there." They followed her through a side door, down a narrow hall, and through another door.

Her rectangular office gave Rick the impression she was organized, but not to the extreme. At one end, next to a small window, stood her wood desk with a computer, telephone, a gooseneck lamp, and a few papers. No books, but who needs them when there are so many in the other rooms? A table and six chairs took up most of the rest of the space, though a single bookshelf stood against one wall, with only a few books, and stacked horizontally. Otherwise, except for a small bronze statuette, it was bare. The only item which could be considered decorative, except for the statuette, was a large photograph of Bassano under snow, its covered bridge in the center bringing memories of the previous evening into Rick's mind. Gisa motioned to a short stack of papers on the table.

"Sit down and I'll tell you what I've found. Not much, I'm afraid, but I don't really know what you're looking for."

"We don't either, Gisa." Betta and Rick sat in the chairs across from their host. Two modern fixtures hung from the high ceiling, lighting the table and the room. "If there is something more about the villa where the paintings were last seen, and if we can pin down whether the Vizentin family lived near it, that might help."

Gisa opened a file and pushed it across. "The villa was never occupied again after the war, and is still in a state of disrepair if not a total shambles. The family line ended in the late 1940s and there was a legal dispute as to the ownership of the property for a decade or so after that, but then everyone seems to have lost interest, and it remains in legal limbo."

Rick studied the papers, running his fingers down the lines. "You've extracted quite a bit of information, Gisa."

"Most of it is from an article written in *Il Mattino di Padova* a couple years ago. I'm not that fast. But I did work on your Vizentin family and found an item which may be of interest. We have a pretty good genealogy section here." She opened the file in front of her. "There are some Vizentins living in the area now, including one older couple in Fossalunga itself." She noticed Rick and Betta exchanging looks. "It appears you knew that already. The others are scattered around the Veneto, but our records don't go too far afield. The family has been around for a while, of course; I found records of births, deaths, marriages, and baptisms dating back to the sixteenth century. But one more recent Vizentin you likely will want to hear about." She pushed a sheet between them and tapped a red fingernail on one line. "Coluccio Vizentin was employed as a gardener at your villa in the late 1930s. I did a general search on him, hoping I would get lucky because of his unusual name, and found that he was listed as a member of a partisan brigade that operated around Bassano in the late years of the war."

Rick put his arm around Betta and gave her a quick squeeze, causing Gisa to raise an eyebrow. "There's our connection, Betta."

"A somewhat tenuous one, you'll have to admit. Half the male population of the region was fighting in the mountains at that time."

"But only Coluccio had a connection to the villa where the paintings disappeared."

Gisa shifted her glance between the two while she listened to their exchange, and then pulled out the last of the files. From it she took a folded piece of thick, and almost ancient, paper. She carefully opened it at the creases, revealing what was likely an architectural drawing of a building. "This is the original floor plan of the villa, if that is of interest to you. Naturally it is anyone's guess where your precious paintings were hung, but most likely it was in one of the public rooms." She pointed to one of the rectangles drawn within the C-shaped structure. "They were on this side, if I understand the writing here, and the sleeping wing is over here." Their eyes followed Gisa's fingers over the yellowed paper. "The kitchens and service quarters were in the back, here."

Rick tapped on the table. "This compass point indicates north, so the windows point south. Is it near a main road?"

Gisa rose to her feet and walked to her desk where she lifted the laptop and brought it back to the table. "I was looking up a satellite view of it just before you got here. Let me get it out of sleep mode." She typed in a password and turned the screen toward Rick and Betta when a screen came to life. "There it is. You can see there is an unpaved road that goes in front of it, but the *strada provinciale* that connects Bassano with Padova is about two kilometers south. It was likely put in after the war and the older road probably fell out of use since it doesn't serve any purpose except to get to and from the villa."

Betta nodded. "A villa that nobody needed to visit."

Drumming his fingers on the table, Rick said, "I know we won't find anything, certainly not the missing Jacopos, but do you think it might be fun to return to the scene of the crime?"

"I was thinking the same thing," Betta replied.

Gisa smiled. "You two make a good team. But promise me you'll be careful."

◇◇◇

Lunch was minimal. They stopped in a bar in Fossalunga and ordered two ham and cheese *pannini* with glasses of mineral water. Rick contained his urge to quiz the proprietor about the Vizentin family, but he did ask about the villa and got nothing. The man had just bought the bar after moving from Padova, and knew little about the town and its surroundings. He might as well have been from Naples. Rick picked a small tube of *Baci* off the counter display when he ordered their coffees, and they split the chocolates as they drank. When they realized it was an odd number in the tube, he insisted Betta have the last one. Hazelnut and dark chocolate—the surest way to a woman's heart.

After tightening the chin straps of their helmets they swung their legs over the Ducati, and Betta brought it to life. Coming out of the town they jogged to the north and turned onto a very straight road on very flat terrain. It was the Via Postumia, an ancient Roman consular road that connected Genoa with the Adriatic Sea, and the Romans didn't like bends. Not only was it straight, it was smooth, since—fortunately for Rick and Betta—it had been re-paved since construction in 144 BC. They turned off the highway after only a few kilometers, crossed a small bridge, and drove onto a small road that was in less than ideal condition. Betta slowed down and skillfully managed to avoid most of the cracks and potholes. But as bad as that pavement was, it was like an airplane runway compared to the rutty dirt road that came next. It bounced and bumped them out of the flat land and up a small hill until they came to their destination.

The hill on which the villa sat was dotted with rocks and weeds, the former likely the reason no one had gone to the trouble to take ownership of the land. Even if someone wanted to develop the land, it would have been a labor of Hercules to move the rocks and boulders from the dirt. And then, what would grow there? Grapes for wine? Rick was not an agronomist, but he thought it unlikely. Even the weeds didn't look healthy.

The path up to the building wove through many of the larger boulders, but it was so overgrown with scrubby bushes that they decided to leave the motorcycle and walk the final meters. As they got closer they could see that the tall windows were without panes of glass, and many window frames had simply disappeared. Had there been curtains, they would now be flapping in the wind, but they were long gone. The architecture was similar to the Rinaldi villa only in that the essential shape was horizontal and long. Any ornamentation had been removed years, perhaps decades, ago. What remained was a shell, like a once-elegant stretch limousine now rusting on blocks. Betta and Rick reached the doorway and set down their helmets.

"Perhaps we should put them back on before going in," suggested Betta.

"I don't see any signs indicating that it's a hard hat area." He pushed open the front door, expecting an eerie creaking sound like in a horror movie, but was disappointed. "According to Gisa's floor plan, the entertaining areas, if that's the word, are off to the left. Let's look there first." They passed into what had been an entrance hall and through an opening where doors once must have hung. The room's emptiness, rather than echoing their steps, muffled them. They stopped in the middle and looked up where a few tatters of paint still stuck to the ceiling and a bare wire hung from a small hole. Rick gestured at the wall opposite the windows. "The paintings might have hung there, to keep the direct sun off them. If they worried about such things in those days." They continued into the next room and found the same emptiness, but here leaves and dirt had blown through the pane-less windows, building little mounds in the four corners. A section of the ceiling had fallen in, and they could feel the outside air being pulled through the windows and up into the hole.

"Look at that, Riccardo." She was pointing to a faint trace of footprints in the dirt. "I wonder how long ago that person was in here."

Rick walked over and knelt down to get a closer look. "Hard to know. It could have been yesterday or last week or last month. It depends on the wind coming through this room, and how long it takes the blowing dirt to cover things up."

She took a breath and folded her arms across her chest. "By one theory, your English friend already has the paintings, so it wouldn't be him. That leaves the German. He could have been poking around here."

Rick got to his feet. "Why would he be looking for them if his grandfather took them? No, I doubt if either of them was here, unless it was to see where the paintings had been when they were stolen. That's what we're doing."

Betta looked at the open window and frowned. "What's that?"

"What?"

"Something's written on the wall."

They scuffed through the dust and peered at a section of the wall next to the window. Letters, and a few numbers, were barely visible on the wallpaper, much of which had peeled off. It appeared that they had been written with a very fine pen, but when Rick bent down and ran his fingers across the surface, he found they had been cut into the wall. One long word was followed underneath by other words and numbers.

"I think it's German. I took only one semester, as a requirement, and could never get used to the sounds. Let me see. It looks like *entfernung*. I think that means—"

"Distance," said Betta. "I took more than a semester." She bent to see the other markings. "Barn. Hill. Bridge. And after each one a number, followed by M. Look out there, Riccardo. So you see a barn?"

"No barn."

"Is there a bridge?"

"Way off down the hill we're on, I think it's the one we crossed on the way here."

"Is it about a hundred and twenty-five meters away?"

"I get it, and how far does it say the hill is?"

"Two hundred twenty meters."

"Someone marked off the distances and carved them on the wall—likely with a bayonet—to help the shooters sight their targets. So Germans used this window to hold off the approaching enemy, or be ready to if they appeared. Betta, it could have been Muller's grandfather."

She looked out the huge opening that once held a window, careful not to brush against the dust that was everywhere. "It sounds like you want to make him the villain."

Rick stared out, trying to picture what the view had been like those many years ago when the war broke the silence of the hill. He stood behind Betta and placed his hands on her shoulders. "Not really. In fact I like the man. But we have to go where the clues lead us."

"There are no clues, Riccardo. It was seventy years ago and there were a lot of Germans in this part of Italy then. It proves nothing."

"I suppose you're right." He dropped his hands from her shoulders and put his arms around her waist. She put her hands over his and they stared into the distance before turning to leave.

After walking through the rest of the villa they exited through the same central door, picked up their helmets, and stepped carefully down the path to the parked motorcycle. Rick was still working on his helmet strap when Betta brought the Mostro to life, and he had barely swung his leg over and settled into his seat when she pushed the bike forward and started down the hill at a low speed. They bounced over ruts and bumps before reaching the paved road, which was not much smoother. A few minutes later they crossed the bridge and came to the main highway. There was no traffic, so instead of a full stop she rolled onto the smooth pavement and gunned the engine. The Ducati responded like a huge dog being let out of a cage, and Rick hung on tightly. Betta leaned forward, concentrating on the distance ahead, while Rick bent his head slightly to the left. The motorcycle was growling into second gear when Rick spotted a dark blue sedan waiting on a side road ahead. As they zipped past, it pulled out behind them.

Not him again.

"Betta, we have company," he shouted. "I hate to suggest it, but can you pick up the speed?"

She tilted her head slightly to look into the mirror on the handlebar. "He can never catch me if I don't want him to," she called back. "Let's have some fun."

Rick was about to suggest that it might be better simply to get away from the guy, but at that moment the bike shot ahead, taking the breath from his lungs. He clung to her waist as she alternatively sped up and then slowed down, always keeping an eye on the mirror. Unable to turn around, Rick could only guess where the car was, but he assumed that she was jerking the guy's chain with her fast and slow speeds. This kept up for ten minutes as they raced through a few small villages and kilometers of open countryside. Rick heard the engine drop an octave and noticed a sign for Cittadella fly past. He tilted to one side in order to see around Betta's helmet. The houses were more frequent, though still only one- and two-story buildings. Cittadella was on the list of places he'd wanted to see, since it was one of the most picturesque walled towns in Italy. But he hadn't expected it to be from the back of a motorcycle.

The street was now lined with houses as they left the countryside completely and neared the city itself. It also narrowed, forcing Betta to pull back on the reins. As they got closer to the walls he could see that the street was on a straight line to one of the four city gates, but then he noticed the circular sign indicating do not enter. For an instant Rick thought she was going to ignore the one-way street and enter the city right there, but instead she paused and made a sharp right turn. Rick took advantage of the turn to glance behind and saw that the dark car was about fifty meters back. Cittadella, he knew, was a round city surrounded by an intact wall system. Inside, the two main streets went straight from one gate to the other, crossing in the center, and the other streets were concentric circles inside the circle of high walls. Rick looked to his left as the motorcycle gunned ahead. Between them and the towering walls was a wide moat and an expanse of grass crisscrossed with paths. He noticed a couple strolling below the ramparts when Betta braked and suddenly cut to the left. The narrow street took them across a bridge over the water in the moat and through a set of double gates. Between the gates Rick looked up, half expecting to be drenched with boiling oil, but by then they were through the wall and inside the town.

Betta, thankfully, slowed down. But at the second corner she swerved to the left into one of the narrower side streets, then braked again and made another left until she reached the wall. They rode along it until a stop sign where she actually came to a complete stop.

"I get the sense you've done this before." Rick called out as she revved the engine.

"A few times. He'll never find us on these streets, but he'll waste quite some time trying." She turned left and they shot through the wall and over the moat. Twenty minutes later they were in Bassano.

During the ride the noise made it impossible to talk, but Rick spent the time trying to figure out who the hell was the guy in the dark sedan. And he imagined Betta doing the same. Her comment when they reached the alley behind the gallery confirmed it. She pulled off the helmet and ran her fingers through her short, black hair.

"Someone thinks you got some information from Sarchetti before he was killed, Riccardo, and now they're following you."

"That may be, but if it's the same guy who tried to run us off the road, he did it before I met with Sarchetti. There must be another reason."

"When you figure it out, let me know." She took his helmet and kissed him on the cheek. "I'd better get back to work, there's an artist coming in this afternoon to set up a new exhibit. Thanks for lunch." She stared at him for a moment and then kissed him again, this time on the lips. "Please be careful."

Chapter Twelve

"We need to talk again."

DiMaio's voice betrayed fatigue, even through the cell phone connection. Rick was standing in the uppermost of the city's trio of connecting squares, near the entrance to the museum and the San Francesco church adjacent to it. When the phone rang he'd been considering a quick visit to the church, partly because he enjoyed church architecture, but also so he could write to his mother that he'd been inside. She assumed that he was attending mass regularly and he tried not to disappoint her, even if it meant stretching the truth. But now it appeared that his act of piety, already tenuous, would have to be postponed.

"Of course, Alfredo. Where do you want to meet this time?"

"I'm near Palazzo Sturm. I'll be out front."

"That's the Ceramics Museum. I can be there in five minutes."

He made it, in fact, in less than five minutes. DiMaio stood in the patio in front of the building, staring over a low wall at the covered bridge just up river. When Rick came through the gates he looked up but stayed at the wall. Rick walked to him and they both leaned on the stone of the wall and stared down at the water. As they watched, the sound of voices, singing, male voices, floated up from the bridge.

"The *Alpini*," said DiMaio. "Whenever ex-alpine troops finds themselves on their bridge, they break into song. It must be something they swear on their unit banner to do when they're discharged, but it's a nice tradition for those of us who live here." His eyes stayed on the river. "Better to associate music with the bridge than violence. I wonder how many people, over the centuries, have been thrown from it? Or thrown themselves from it? Our little murder last night could not have been the first." He turned to Rick. "I'm sure you know that this isn't the original bridge. The last time it was destroyed was not in a flood or fire, like the previous times, but with explosives. The partisans blew it up and got three of their own shot in reprisal by the Nazis." He shook his head, as if to signal that the subject was closed. "Have you been in the museum?"

"Not yet, Alfredo, but it's on my list."

"Let's go in, we can talk as we look at the exhibits." They walked across the small courtyard and mounted the steps. Behind an admission desk sat a stocky man with a large red beard and a shock of hair to match it. Rick was about to pull out some euros when the man recognized the policeman and waved them both through.

"A friend of yours, Alfredo?"

"I took a thorn out of his paw a while back. He returns the favor by always letting me in free, not that I come here that often." They walked into a room in which the ornate ceramics in the display cases competed with the even more ornate decoration of the walls and ceiling. "I hope you like rococo."

"I must admit I'm not a big fan."

DiMaio stopped and peered at a large flowered bowl under one of the glass cases. "The style goes with the ceramics, at least in this room." They studied the bowl for a few moments before walking through a doorway to a room with more of the same on walls and display. "But we didn't come here just to talk about decoration. Riccardo, Inspector Occasio is getting more and more frustrated with this case. I know the man well, unfortunately, and if he stays true to form he will lash out. I fear that he may take someone into custody who is not the guilty party."

"You mean me."

"It would not surprise me."

"Listen, Alfredo, Occasio might think I'm some naïve American, but if he'll have his hands full if he tries something with me. You know as well as I do there's no evidence to make me a serious suspect in either of these crimes."

The detective kept his eyes on the displays and did not answer. Once they left the large salon, the other rooms were of smaller and similar size, and the ceramics more recent. "Have you spoken to your uncle?"

It had been in the back of Rick's mind since Occasio and his men had appeared at the hotel. "No, and I don't want him to get involved. You can call it the American in me, but I would rather deal with this myself than lean on family connections."

DiMaio put on the ironic smile with which Rick was now all too familiar. "Very noble of you, Riccardo, and yes, not very Italian. Perhaps once you've been back in Italy long enough you'll change." He took what was either a deep breath or a sigh. "I, of course, will do everything I can to keep Occasio from doing anything rash, but I can't promise I'll be successful."

"I appreciate that, Alfredo. What about all the other suspects? The real ones."

They had wandered into a room with modern, whimsical pieces, including a ceramic table on which everything was also ceramic, including the silverware and food. All the items on the table had an eerie, white glaze, as if it were a banquet set for ghosts.

"He has not told me so specifically, but I believe he has ruled out the prominent people of our community. Your friend's uncle Angelo Rinaldi, for example, as well as the banker, Porcari, and even our museum curator Paolo Tibaldi. They would have had to be caught standing over the bleeding body of our victims before he would take the risk of arresting one of them. Occasio is very careful when dealing with anyone who has power, be it political, bureaucratic, or economic. So that leaves our three foreigners. Randolph, your compatriot, doesn't have a real motive any more than do the others. He is also so engrossed with his *fidanzata* that he wouldn't want to spoil the magic by getting involved in murder. Oglesby, the Brit, seems too disorganized to plan a couple murders. The German is an interesting study, as you'll remember from our interview with him. I just wonder if something went on during his dinner with Sarchetti that he didn't want to tell us. But if he killed Sarchetti, what motive did he have to murder Fortuna?"

They looked silently into one more glass case before Rick spoke. "I know you don't want to hear this, nor does your boss, but I believe that the two murders have something to do with the two missing Jacopo Bassano paintings."

"I've seen this movie before, Riccardo. I didn't like it then and I don't now."

Rick held up his hands. "As you wish. Then how about Gaddi? You didn't mention him."

"The ancient professor? It is highly unlikely that Gaddi would have the desire or certainly the physical strength to commit one murder, let alone two. Even when he told Occasio and me this morning that he'd met with Sarchetti yesterday, the inspector crossed him off the suspect list. The man was shaking like a leaf, and not from guilt."

Rick remembered how strong the professor's handshake had been, but kept that little detail to himself. He wanted to argue for a connection between the murder and the Jacopo paintings, but given DiMaio's strong reaction, he let it go. Also, while he hated to admit it to himself, DiMaio could be right—the murders had nothing to do with Jacopo's work, missing or otherwise.

A few minutes later the two walked down the steps into the open air. As it had the previous day, the sky was darkening and what had been a slight breeze had become a chill wind. Both unconsciously pulled their coats closed. When they reached the gate, the detective's normal face had become somber.

"Riccardo, promise me you'll think about calling your uncle."

The last issue Rick wanted to face at that moment was Erica's pre-marital quandary, but as he walked through the doors into the hotel lobby it raised its head again. This time it was without Erica herself. Randolph spotted Rick, strode to him, and asked—almost pleaded—that he join him in the bar for a chat. It was the last way Rick wanted to spend a few minutes, but there was nothing he could do. After ordering for both of them, the professor got down to business.

"Erica has gone for a walk, Rick. She seems to be doing that a lot since she arrived here. And she's been moody too. At first I thought it was the fatigue of jet lag, but I'm wondering if there's more to it."

Oh, boy, thought Rick. "Jet lag always wipes me out too, Jeff. I usually figure a day for each hour of time difference to get used to the new time zone. She's only been here a few days."

"I hope you're right." Randolph stared into his drink, a draft beer. Rick did the same with his *Crodino*. "But you know, Rick, there is an age difference between the two of us."

Rick nodded but kept silent. He couldn't really say that he hadn't noticed.

"Since you knew Erica before…before she came to the States, I thought you could give me your thoughts. Man to man."

Rick wasn't ready for another sip of his drink, but he took one to give him time to figure out an answer. What could he say? It came to him. "It may be a cultural thing, Jeff."

"A cultural thing?"

"Right. She's thrust into another culture, and let me tell you, you can't underestimate the difficulty of adapting to a new country. I've seen it dozens of times with Americans coming over to Italy. At first they love it—all the food, history, and art. But then they start to feel homesick. Some little thing touches it off, like not being able to find a good cheeseburger or an encounter with a shop-keeper that doesn't understand English. They go into a funk. The same thing can happen to foreigners who have moved to America. I saw it with an Italian friend of mine at the university."

"So Erica is going through culture shock?" He grinned and took a long pull of his beer as his mind worked on the concept. "She comes back for the first time and is reminded of what she left behind. What has been welling up inside her for months comes rushing out. 'Have I done the right thing?' she asks herself."

"Uh, sure. That could be happening."

"So it may not be the idea of getting married. Or me."

Rick gave Randolph as noncommittal a shrug as he could muster and swallowed some more from his glass. It was the last. "Jeff, I'm glad we had this chance to talk, but I have a telephone appointment set up with a client in New Mexico. Can't be late for it." He reached for his wallet.

Randolph waved him off. "Don't be silly, I invited you. And thank you for letting me bend your ear." He shook Rick's hand warmly and allowed him to escape. As he left the bar Rick wondered once again if he'd done the right thing.

When he reached the reception desk the clerk looked up from his computer. "Signor Montoya, a message was left for you." The clerk turned around, retrieved an envelope from the rows of boxes behind him, and handed it over with the room key.

Rick pulled open the envelope and wondered, in the era of cell phones, who would be leaving a handwritten note. It came to him as he unfolded the paper, and its contents confirmed his hunch. SOMETHING HAS COME UP. MEET ME AT 6:00 AT VIA LOMBARDIA 11. It was signed Fabio Innocenti. So the old man has found something regarding the two missing Jacopos. The break they needed may have finally appeared, and it turned out to be Betta's father who caught the break. He checked the clock behind the desk and realized it was almost six.

"Is Via Lombardia nearby?"

The clerk smiled as he pulled out a map. "It is in the *centro storico*, so it is very close." His finger ran over the map and stopped. "Right here. About ten minutes away—on foot, of course." The phone buzzed below the counter and the clerk answered it. As he listened he looked up at Rick. "Just a moment, I'll check," he said into the phone before putting the call on hold and turning back to Rick. "It's the *questura*, Signor Montoya. Inspector Occasio is requesting that you call immediately."

From the way the man pronounced the title of the policeman, Rick sensed that Occasio had not made a friend during his visits to the hotel. "Please tell him I just left and you'll leave a message to call him."

The clerk smiled and spoke to the person on the line before putting down the phone. Rick looked up again at the clock, thanked the man, and handed back his room key. He started toward the door but stopped halfway across the lobby, pulling out his cell phone and hitting a few buttons. The call went to voice mail, causing a frown of annoyance to appear on Rick's face. He sat in one of the lobby chairs and intently tapped in a message before hitting SEND. He put the phone back in his pocket and strode toward the door.

Early evening was already spreading over the sky. A layer of clouds had pushed the darkness into making an early arrival while bringing the possibility of more rain. The people on the streets, more savvy to the vagaries of local weather, sensed this and scurried toward their destinations. He thought he heard a roll of thunder, but it might have been the sound of a motorbike a few streets away. That made him think of Betta and her brother's motorcycle and then of her father. What could the old man have found? He hoped it was something that might cast some light on the mystery of the missing paintings, but he didn't want to get his hopes up. There wasn't a single expert in the seminar who thought they would ever see those two masterpieces, so who was Rick to dispute them?

He turned off onto Via Lombardia, which was more of an alley than a street. The large, metal trash cans—almost mini-dumpsters—that Italian municipalities used sat at various angles near the doorways. These were the back doors of apartments or businesses which would have more ornate façades on the opposite side of their buildings. What would bring Innocenti to a street like this? Something wasn't right. A memory jumped into his head—a narrow dirt street in a rough part of southwest Albuquerque. That night had not ended well. He blocked out the thought, but a tinge of fear remained and his breaths shortened.

The pavement was narrow, but a few small cars were wedged close enough to the buildings to allow others to pass. He checked

the numbers as he passed. Fortunately there was still enough light
to see them, though it was fading fast. Number eleven would be
close to the end of the block.

The door was ajar. Rick pushed it and peered into a room
filled with what appeared to be office supplies. Lights on the
walls illuminated the scene. Cleaning equipment, including
mops and buckets, had been pushed into one corner next to a
sink. Beside the sink sat three large bins marked with triangular
recycling symbols. Two were empty, the other overflowing with
shredded paper. About a dozen boxes of supplies lined a set of
metal shelves or were stacked neatly on the floor.

"Signor Innocenti?" His voice wavered.

There was no answer, but he thought he heard something
coming from the far corner. He walked toward it and found
another door, also slightly ajar. He pushed it open and stepped
into another room that was well lit by a large overhead fixture,
its light glaring off the tiled floor. A shelf on one side of the
room held more boxes of supplies, but also two paintings whose
style was strikingly familiar to Rick. His heartbeat quickened.
Sitting in a wood chair opposite the two works sat a man who
now turned his attention to Rick. As he did, he lifted a pistol
from his lap and aimed it at Rick's chest.

"You were expecting someone else, Mister Montoya?" Stefano
Porcari's face showed indifference but then broke into a grim
smile. "Don't be alarmed that Innocenti may be in any danger,
Riccardo, he and his lovely daughter are safe. It is only you who
have gotten yourself into this predicament."

"What kind of predicament, Signor Porcari? Did you think
I was coming to rob your bank?"

"That is exactly what I think. How good of you to come to
that conclusion so quickly. I trust Inspector Occasio will do the
same when the evidence is handed to him on a silver platter."

Rick surveyed the room and felt his palms beginning to sweat.
Next to Porcari were more boxes, these with stenciled mark-
ing for the Banco di Bassano. Forms, Rick guessed; all banks
needed forms. This must be the rear part of the bank building,

the storage area. Otherwise, except for the two paintings, the room was bare save a pointed metal object on one of the boxes next to the chair.

"I'm sorry that I do not have another chair for you, Riccardo, but the floor will serve when the time comes."

The room was not large. Rick calculated that the banker was about a dozen feet from him, too far to charge and get away with it. He would get Porcari's eyes somewhere other than on him, so he could edge closer.

"I suppose you think I was going to steal those paintings." He gestured at the two framed works on the shelf and the banker glanced at them. Rick moved a few inches toward him.

"Those paintings? You could have had them just by asking." He stared at the bright colors on the two, as if in a trance. Rick inched closer. "They are the reason all of this started, my dear Riccardo. Look at those wonderful masterpieces. But of course you know all about them, Sarchetti told you at the bridge."

Rick couldn't keep from looking. What did the man mean? What did Porcari think that Sarchetti had told him? "Sarchetti told me nothing about any paintings at the bridge. I don't understand what you mean."

"That charlatan sells me these pieces of trash and then gets drunk and brags about it. I know that's what happened." He turned his attention back to Rick, who had managed to move an inch closer, but still not close enough. The gun moved back and forth in the man's hand. "That's of no consequence now. Everything will work out for the best. Who would have thought that the interpreter would be the murderer of two men? Perhaps you learned such skills in America. Such a violent country."

The words drove home the fact that this was a man who must have killed two men already. This time it would be with a gun and not a knife. Rick concentrated on his plan. It was the only way to save himself. "Why would the police think I was a murderer, Signor Porcari?" He was stalling for time, but the situation did not look promising.

The narrow smile returned to the banker's face. "It's too perfect. You break into the bank to steal paintings like those that you admired on the walls of my office. I happened to have mentioned to you, when you visited, that I had two new masterpieces in our storage area." He noticed the frown on Rick's face. "Of course I neglected to say that when we had coffee, but the police will believe me. Inspector Occasio considers me the very picture of honesty."

Rick's breaths were coming shorter now as he understood Porcari's plan and realized the genius of it. The banker, aware of his guest's discomfort, smiled and continued.

"The security cameras near the outer door will show you entering. And the door has been jimmied open by nothing less that the knife that killed Sarchetti." He waved his hand over what Rick now realized was a short, wood-handled dagger. "Your fingerprints will be on it, of course. And I, working late, heard noises in the back of the bank, and came to investigate. Fortunately, I am armed with this gun which I have a license to carry. We law-abiding citizens must be sure to follow the rules, and you know that we always have to be prepared for an attempted bank robbery. Usually the thieves are after cash, but why not paintings?"

"You thought everything out, Signor Porcari. But one part of all this I don't understand."

"The least I can do for you, Riccardo, given this final service you are about to perform for me, is clear up any misunderstandings. What is it?"

"Why did you have to kill Fortuna?"

The question caused Porcari to shake, making Rick regret the question, even if it bought him a few precious seconds. The gun wavered while remaining trained on Rick's chest.

"The man would have ruined me," he said through clenched teeth. "That's all you need to know." He lifted the gun with unsteady hands.

Rick raised his hands defensively, in a reflex movement, when Betta screamed behind him. Porcari's head jerked toward the doorway and Rick leaped at him. The chair collapsed under the weight of the two men, but Rick grabbed the wrist that held the gun and forced it up. He was surprised by the strength he felt in the man's arm.

"Betta, get out of here!"

His voiced was drowned out by shots from the waving pistol. Two bullets slammed into the opposite wall as the men struggled on the floor. Rick kept his two hands on the man's wrist, pushing the gun away, but the banker had better leverage, gripping it firmly while pressing the barrel back toward Rick. Porcari growled as his free hand struck out at Rick's face, punching him above the eye. A few drops of blood dripped into the corner of the left eye, blurring his vision. The man was on top of Rick, pulling the fist back for a second punch, when his arms sagged limp and surprise stiffened his face into a grimace. He groaned in pain and the gun clattered to the floor. Rick shoved the man off, grabbed the pistol, and got himself to his feet. He was ready to aim at Porcari, but immediately saw that the man was no longer a threat. The knife protruded from Porcari's shoulder and he gasped in pain. Betta stood above him, arms taut, breathing heavily.

"A doctor…a doctor. You must help me." Porcari clutched at his bleeding back but the knife was just out of reach. As he twisted in pain the weapon dislodged by itself and hit the tiles with a metal clank.

Betta kicked it expertly to the other side of the room, far from the man's reach. "It doesn't look that serious. I've had worse injuries falling off a motorcycle. Keep that gun ready, Riccardo."

Rick trained the pistol on Porcari with one hand and pulled out his cell phone with the other. "I'll call DiMaio."

"No need, I already did when I got your message on my phone. I knew my father wasn't planning on meeting you and the address was strange, so it smelled like a trap. With two dead bodies already, I thought you shouldn't take any chances."

They kept their eyes on Porcari as they talked, oblivious to his short, groaning breaths. "Did you tell DiMaio that you were coming here yourself?"

"He didn't ask, so I didn't tell him." She gave Rick a quick grin. "He would not have approved, and if I hadn't come, where would you be now?"

Rick nodded, and watched Porcari writhe on the cold tiles. "You've got a point, Betta." They both looked up when the faint sound of a police siren made its way into the room. "DiMaio and the cavalry."

"Riccardo, look at that!"

Rick tensed and his eyes jerked down to Porcari. "What?"

She was staring at the shelf with the two paintings. "The missing Jacopos, the cause of all this, and now they're damaged." She walked to the shelf and raised her finger to touch the bullet holes. One was almost in the center of the left painting, the other at a corner of the second. "Was he aiming at them? They make it intact through wars and revolutions and now, after all those centuries, this happens."

Rick shook his head. "Unless I've got everything completely wrong, Betta, those two paintings are not our missing Jacopos. They are—" The sound of brakes, doors slamming and feet in the outer store room cut off his sentence. DiMaio appeared in the doorway, stopped, and took in the scene.

"I thought you'd never get here, Alfredo. Did you stop for a coffee on the way?"

◇◇◇

Rather than the deluge of the previous day, only a few thick drops splashed over Bassano as Rick and Betta walked slowly along the stone street, her shoulder tucked under his arm. Bassano's good citizens, expecting the rain, were now nowhere to be seen except for an occasional soul hurrying home. The street lights had been on for an hour, but their rays did not reach into the darkened doorways of this narrow lane that was mostly shops and offices, now closed for the day. They had not spoken since leaving behind the flashing lights of the police cars on Via Lombardia, but now Rick felt Betta breathe a deep sigh and knew she was ready.

"How can you be sure that those are not the missing Jacopos?"

She could not see his smile. "I wondered how long it would take you to ask. Those two works had been sold to Porcari by Sarchetti, he as much as told me so when he trained the gun on my chest. But Fortuna told him they were fake. Porcari knew that the nasty professor would have broadcast to everyone that he had spotted the forgeries. The banker would have been exposed as having used bank money to buy forgeries, which would have ended his career at Banco di Bassano and eliminated his chances of working in any other bank. Just as bad, the man's reputation among art collectors was ruined. Fortuna had to go. As did Sarchetti, for having sold him fakes in the first place. And when he thought Sarchetti had told me about the whole affair, I was going to be next."

Betta stared at the pavement, a frown crimping her red lips. "I got that, but what you haven't explained is why you believe that the two damaged paintings couldn't have been our missing Jacopos."

"I might be wrong, but I think the two Jacopos, had they been offered to Porcari, would have been outside the bank's price range. He told me as much when I visited him at the bank."

"So they remain missing. The mystery continues."

"I have a hunch about who has them."

The comment had the expected effect, Betta stopped short and turned to face Rick. "What? Riccardo Montoya, you tell me everything this instant."

"You sound like my mother." He tousled her hair. "Let me check something out after I drop you off. I don't want to give you my theory and then have it turn out to be my imagination. One way or another, I'll tell you everything when we have dinner."

She reached up and patted the bandage above his eye. "Are you sure you don't need that looked at by a doctor?"

"Now that you have touched it, the healing is complete."

"What a romantic scene." The slurred voice growled from a darkened doorway before the man lurched out into the street, blocking their way. He wore a dark suit under a leather coat, his tie knot loose and askew.

Betta clutched Rick's arm. "It's my ex-fiancé."

"We've met." *I hope this one isn't armed.*

Chapter Thirteen

"Carlo, you're drunk." Betta clutched Rick's arm. "Go home, you'll get yourself in trouble."

The man swayed slightly and his eyes shifted between Rick and Betta. "And who will give me any trouble? Certainly not him."

Rick watched Carlo's body swaying before him and noticed the bloodshot eyes, making it easy to size up the situation. If he were careful he should not have much trouble with the guy. He had successfully faced bigger challenges in Albuquerque bars, and many of those weren't as drunk as Carlo. So why not tie up some loose ends? His hands dropped to his sides and he rubbed his palms slowly along his coat. "Is this what you do for Porcari, follow people around?"

Carlo's body stiffened, like he'd just been slapped. It was just the reaction Rick had hoped for. "What I do at the bank is of no interest to you."

"It is if you become a danger to other drivers."

Betta looked up at Rick. "What do you mean?"

Rick kept his eyes on the unsteady figure before them. "Carlo knows what I mean. You were trailing Sarchetti for your boss weren't you?" There was no response. "But then you saw Bettta and me on the motorcycle, and that got your interest, didn't it? You decided to follow me instead."

"What I do for the bank is no business of yours," he repeated. He was obviously clenching and unclenching his fists.

"You said that already. You even got up early to see where I went jogging. Someone could have been hurt."

"Riccardo, what do you—?"

"I'll explain later, Betta. I want Carlo to know that what he's been up to the last few days hasn't gone unobserved."

"My boss will—"

"Your boss is on his way to jail, Carlo. He won't be able to help even his most loyal employee. Now go home as Betta suggested."

Rick knew what was coming and had planned to react. Carlo stepped forward and pulled back his fist to strike. Rick smacked him in the knee with his boot with a cracking sound. The man howled in pain, giving Rick a look of hate just as Rick's fist caught him square in the jaw. He crumpled to the ground.

"Let's get you home, Betta, Carlo will be a while getting up."

A slurred shout reached their ears, but they were too far away from the man on the pavement to understand it. Betta squeezed Rick's arm as they turned the corner. Later, as they walked into Piazza Monte Vecchio, Rick was still answering Betta's questions. "I didn't want to worry you. The wire was a nasty prank, but nothing came of it, and at that point I didn't know if it was intended for me or Caterina. The way she reacted, not wanting the police to be told, makes me think that she's into something nasty herself."

Betta stopped and looked up at the lighted windows of her father's apartment. "Will we ever find out about Caterina? This morning my father was wondering the same thing."

"The mystery woman. My guess is that she's returned to Milan after the excitement of her morning's run, and we'll never know what she's really been up to."

Betta slipped her arm inside Rick's coat and around his waist. Her hands were cold, but he didn't complain. "Riccardo, this sounds terrible, but all this excitement has given me an appetite."

"A bowl of pasta does sound good. I have something to do at the hotel but then I'll be back. Think about where you'd like to dine."

"And you will tell me your theories about the missing Jacopos."

By then, they may not be theories.

◇◇◇

The hotel lobby was deserted except for one person sitting in a chair on the far side. Unfortunately for Rick it was Erica, and as usual she was dressed perfectly. She stood and waved, and he reluctantly walked to her and planted the required kisses on her cheeks. There was that perfume again. He noticed that her smile was brighter than he'd seen it since she'd barged back into his life. Had it only been a couple days?

"Come sit with me for a moment, Ricky. I have something to tell you."

"Sure, but for just a minute."

He sat down next to her on the sofa and was surprised when she took his hand in hers. "Ricky, I have decided to stay with Jeffrey." Rick opened his mouth to speak but she held up her hand to stop him. "But what I want to tell you is that I couldn't have made the decision without your help."

"Erica, I did nothing."

"Oh, yes you did. I will always be grateful." She squeezed his hand. "Jeffrey has been pushing me to set a wedding date, and now we will. Sometime before the summer, I think. You will be invited, of course. You'll come, won't you? He wants to rent a villa in Tuscany and invite all our friends from the States. Destination weddings in Italy are very much in vogue these days, but I'm thinking Umbria. Tuscany has been overdone. "

The woman will never change.

"Erica, that's great news, and it will be an honor to be invited to the big event, wherever it takes place. Listen, I really must go. Dinner appointment. Give my best to Jeff." He got to his feet. "*Ciao, bella,*" he said before walking off. "*Tanti auguri.*" Though it might be Jeff who needs the good luck, he thought as he approached the reception desk. Erica was making the right decision, but probably for the wrong reasons. Still, if the outcome was the correct one, did it really matter? That's the question—was it truly the correct decision?

His mind moved quickly to the next issue at hand. The clerk looked up from his computer, passed over the room key without being asked, and returned to the screen. Rick weighed the heavy metal number in his hand before getting the clerk's attention.

"Is Professor Gaddi in his room?"

The clerk checked the various cubicles. "His key is out, so he should be. If you'd like to call him it's room 214."

"*Grazie.*" Rick walked past the niche where the house phone sat and continued to the elevator. He got off at the second floor and walked past several doors before reaching the right one. After taking a breath he rapped twice. He heard footsteps and then a voice.

"*Chi è?*"

"Riccardo Montoya, Professor."

When the door opened Rick was struck by Gaddi's appearance, beginning with the man's hollow eyes. They looked like they hadn't seen sleep for days, and the stubble on his face added to the haunted look. A tie hung loose from the frayed open collar of his wrinkled shirt. The smile was forced, for appearances' sake.

"Riccardo, I was not expecting visitors. Let me invite you in. Fortunately they have given me a room which allows me to do so. Two chairs, if you can believe it." He stood back to allow his visitor to enter. The small sitting area had the chairs as well as a television that was tuned to the national news. The usual generic mountain scenes were framed on the wall. Beyond another doorway would be the bedroom and a bath. Rick thanked him and took a seat.

"We are still under house arrest, Riccardo." He rubbed his chin as if just realizing its need for a razor. "Let me turn off the news, there's nothing that will cheer us up." He pressed the remote that had been sitting on the table between them and the screen went dark. When he put it back down he noticed the glass of wine on the table. "Can I offer you some wine, Riccardo? It's from the little refrigerator, so it's not the finest."

"No thank you, Professor."

"And what brings you here, Riccardo? To share the misery of our forced confinement? Bassano is a lovely town, but not when one is required to remain in it." He picked up the glass and brought it to his lips.

"The forced confinement has come to an end, Professor. The murderer of the two men has been apprehended."

The glass, still full, returned to the table. "Really? *Grazie a dio*. I shall be able to return home. How do you know?"

Rick saw no reason not to recount the scene in the bank warehouse, though he did not go into detail about the struggle. He watched Gaddi carefully when he came to the part about the two paintings, now each with a bullet hole. The professor listened and sipped his wine.

"You were fortunate to get away safely, Riccardo. But how strange that Porcari would have resorted to such violence. It makes sense now that you've tied everything together, but I would never have suspected him." He studied the ruby liquid in his glass, lost in thought.

"My friend Betta thinks that the two paintings are the missing Jacopos."

Gaddi came out of his trance. "Does she?"

Rick leaned forward. "But I do not think either of those paintings is a Jacopo, Professor. And I believe you don't either."

The weary cast of Gaddi's face was now mixed with sadness. The two men looked at each other in silence, broken after a few moments by the older man. "I don't understand what you mean, Riccardo." The indignation in his voice, if that's what is was, appeared forced.

"I saw Sarchetti last night after dinner, before he was killed, and he was in high spirits. The visit to Bassano had gone surprisingly well, he told me, without going into details. But since he was a businessman who dealt in buying and selling art, my assumption was that he had made a deal, and a very lucrative one. Today Detective DiMaio mentioned in passing that you had met with Sarchetti yesterday afternoon." Gaddi's face remained unchanged. Rick continued. "My friend Betta's name is Innocenti. She works with her father at their gallery in Piazza Monte Vecchio, Arte Innocenti." A flicker of something appeared in the old man's eyes. "You went to the gallery and made some vague inquiries about buying and selling art. I found that curious. But it started to make sense when I heard about your meeting with Sarchetti. I had always found it strange that the man was at the seminar in the first place, but now it all comes together. What better place to meet to talk about selling paintings by Jacopo Bassano than at a seminar about the master himself?"

Rick watched as Gaddi got to his feet, walked slowly to the other side of the room, and stopped. He spoke to Rick but his eyes were somewhere else. "Riccardo, two memories of my childhood have stayed with me all my life, and they both deal with my father. The first was his activities in the war. He was barely a teenager when he slipped out of his home in Padova and joined the partisans. He never wanted to talk about it, even when I asked him. It was that way until he died. But my uncles filled me in, and at the funeral I met many of the men he'd fought beside, one of whom told me how my father saved his life."

Gaddi walked to the table and took a long drink of the wine while Rick waited. "My other memory is of my father's love for art. Where he acquired it I never discovered, but since he worked in a factory, everything he knew was self-taught. He was certainly not a rich man, but he collected whenever he could, and our home was filled with color. I would sit in front of a painting on a small stool and he would tell me about it—the use of color, the composition, the symbolism. When I am in front of a class I always think of those times. The love of art was what he passed on to me, and I made it my life work. He died after I got my first professorship and taught my first class. I remember him sitting in the back of the lecture hall."

The old man swallowed hard and did not meet Rick's eyes. He stayed on his feet.

"One day when I was about ten, I got into the attic of our house. I had been told never to go up there alone, since it was dark, dusty, and dirty, but like any child I was curious. Among all the old furniture, boxes, and books was an ancient trunk. I thought it would have treasure or something equally valuable, and when I opened it I found two paintings wrapped in cloth. They were beautiful works, even at that age I could recognize it. The next day I wanted to ask my father about them, why they weren't on the walls with our others, but I knew I would be in trouble if he found out that I had gone to the attic by myself.

"I forgot about it, grew up, went to the university and started my profession. It was only when my mother died and I was forced to go through my parents' belongings that I got into the attic again and again came upon that trunk. By that time I had taken on Jacopo da Bassano as one of my specialties, and when I unwrapped the cloth from the two paintings I realized what I had in my hands."

For the first time since starting his story, Gaddi looked directly at Rick. "But I also realized how the paintings had come into my father's hands. My emotions were a mixture of elation and shame. For weeks I wrestled with myself over what to do, and I finally decided that my father's reputation was more important than returning the two works to the world of art. So I kept them, knowing that some day it would all have to come out, but long after my father was gone."

He walked out of the room and Rick could hear water running in the bathroom sink. Gaddi returned with a filled glass and set it down next to the now-empty wineglass. Rick waited as the man put his thoughts together to continue.

"Last year my wife became ill. I believe I told you about that when we met at the museum. When she could not be cured by our local doctors, I became desperate. They told me there was a specialist in Switzerland who might be able to help, if I could get the money together from friends and relatives. I knew that would be impossible, but I remembered the two Jacopos. I made some discreet inquiries, without revealing anything, and was told about Franco Sarchetti. I contacted him and we agreed to meet here in Bassano."

Rick waited a few moments to be sure that the professor had finished. "From what I've heard about Sarchetti's reputation, he was probably the perfect man for the sale."

Gaddi returned to his chair and took a sip of water. His voice now was hoarse. "He knew he had me over a barrel, and I'm sure he had some prospective buyers in mind. In that meeting yesterday we finally settled on a price. It would have taken care of my wife's treatment, but I'm convinced it was a small fraction of the true value of the two. What made me most ashamed was that these masterpieces might never see the light of day again. They'd be prisoners in the private collection of some millionaire. For a scholar, that was like a knife in the heart." Rick was about to speak, but Gaddi held up his hand. "Let me show you. You will understand." He walked into the other room and Rick could hear a door opening, then closing. When he returned, Gaddi was carrying a long, thin suitcase. He laid it on the carpet and pulled a zipper that went around three sides. Carefully he opened the flap and removed two cloth sacks. His hands were shaking as he pulled the two painting from the sacks and set them against the wall.

Rick had seen slides of Jacopo's works during the seminar and looked at them up close at the museum, but being with these two in a small room made him feel like he was almost with the master in his workshop. Rick wanted to be excited. It should have been a special privilege to study two paintings that had not seen the light of day for more than half a century. But as he focused on the two works, he felt sadness and guilt. The man before him had been put in the terrible position of choosing between the ethics of his life work and saving the woman he loved. The truth about what Gaddi had done would have come to light eventually, Rick knew that. He only wished he hadn't been the one to make it happen. Why couldn't Captain Scuderi have appeared on the scene when needed? Rick pushed the thoughts to the back of his mind and concentrated on the paintings.

Jacopo's genius flowed out from the canvases with movement and color. Both had religious themes, but the biblical stories they told were too obscure for Rick to recognize them. The scenes were filled with people and animals coexisting in harmony, as if the religious subject was merely a pretext for the artist to create an idyllic representation of rural life. Rick learned at the seminar that Jacopo was a man who remained loyal to his roots, and especially to his hometown. He had never left Bassano for any long period, despite the temptations of Venice and other larger cities. It was here that he'd raised his family, teaching his sons to paint and carry on the tradition. Rick's eye moved from the figures to the landscape behind them, wondering how many of the hills and mountains were the same that surrounded the town today. He knew it would be a question that Jacopo scholars would debate in the future, though after this seminar the art community should let Jacopo rest in peace for a few years. Two murders, a man in prison, and another man's career in jeopardy. Was it all worth it for works of art? He studied the two canvases in an attempt to get an answer, knowing there would be none. He was so immersed in them that he almost forgot that Gaddi was in the same room.

"They are magnificent, Professor. I understand completely how painful your decision must have been. These paintings should be displayed where anyone can see them."

Gaddi barely heard Rick's remark. His head was in his hands. "Sarchetti was my last chance to save Pina. What will I do now? Not only will I not have the money for her treatment, I will be arrested for hiding stolen artwork."

Rick extended his hand to touch the man's shoulder but then pulled it back, taking a deep breath. After another gaze at the paintings he reached into his pocket, took out his cell phone, and punched in a number. It took four rings before it was answered.

"Beppo? I've got something for you."

Chapter Fourteen

"I was sure Inspector Occasio would be with you so that he could personally thank me for tying up his murder investigation."

DiMaio and Rick looked out over the Brenta, its ripples catching the reflection of the spotlights trained on the bridge. They could hear the faint sound of the early newscast from one of the houses that lined the riverbank close to where they stood. Perhaps the murder was already being reported since there had been a crew setting up on the street when Rick and Betta slipped out of the warehouse.

"I'm certain the inspector would have sent his warmest thanks had he known I was going to be seeing you, Riccardo. You must forgive me for neglecting to mention it to him. He was extremely busy trying to sort out the details to his advantage."

"The poor man will no longer have a contact in the bank."

"*Al contrario*, my friend. When I left Occasio, he was talking with the bank president himself, no doubt assuring him that he would be doing all he could to contain the scandal."

Rick leaned his elbows on the railing. "That may be tough to do with Porcari taken off in handcuffs."

"My *capo* will find a way, I assure you. But enough about him. Now that you are no longer a suspect, we can return to the issue of your future in the police."

Rick chuckled. "There will be none, my friend. I am perfectly happy to work occasionally on the periphery. Keep in mind, if I had been a cop this week I would have had to take orders from the inspector."

DiMaio nodded as he stared at the light far down the river. "I have no way to respond to such an argument, Riccardo. But let me say that it has been a pleasure to work with you this week, even if you were on the periphery."

Rick turned and examined the policeman's face. "Are you turning serious on me, Alfredo? After all you've done to earn my esteem?"

"Sorry, I don't know what came over me. But let me stay serious for a moment longer and ask if, when you see your uncle, you could put in a word for me. I have put in for a transfer, you see, and—"

"You want to break up your partnership with Occasio? I'm dumbfounded. It would be like Holmes without Watson, Poirot without Hastings, Nero without Archie—"

"Or Laurel without Hardy. I see your point, Riccardo, but I'm ready for a change. So if you mention this to your uncle, I would be eternally grateful. But I should not keep you. I trust you are dining with your lady friend?"

"Incredible. You policemen know everything even before it happens. Yes, since she saved my life, the very least I can do is take her to dinner."

◇◇◇

Rick walked slowly through the wet streets toward Betta's apartment. The adrenalin from the encounter with Porcari had subsided, leaving only negative thoughts, especially when he recalled the events of the past few days. Two men had died. He'd come close to physical harm, but worse yet he'd put Betta in danger as well. Caterina had barely escaped serious injury. And now the question of Professor Gaddi was eating away at him. Had he done the right thing? He was ready to get out of Bassano and return to the relative calm of Rome and his translation business, but that meant leaving Betta, the one bright spot in all of this. How ironic that Rome would seem idyllic in comparison with the sleepy town of Bassano.

He turned the corner and entered Piazza Monte Vecchio. There was only one light on in Betta's apartment, but her father's was lit up. That would make sense, Rick thought, she is telling her father about everything that had happened. Knowing how protective Innocenti tried to be of his daughter, he hoped the man was taking it well and that he wouldn't blame Rick for getting her into harm's way. He reached the doorway and pressed the button under Betta's name. When there was no answer he hit that of the other apartment, and a few seconds later her voice came over the *citofono.*

"Come on up, Riccardo."

She sounded in good spirits. The door buzzed open, and he climbed the stairs to where she stood at the open door of her father's apartment. They had left each other a half hour earlier but they exchanged kisses anyway. She had sprayed on fresh perfume and once again he tried unsuccessfully to identify it. Was he losing his touch?

"I think you'll be pleased to find that we have a guest." A pixie smile matched perfectly with her short hair. She took his coat and laid it over a chair in the small hallway before they walked into the living room. Sitting on the sofa across from Signor Innocenti was Caterina Savona, as always dressed impeccably. The two looked up at him with more smiles, and Innocenti rose to his feet to shake Rick's hand before gesturing at Caterina.

"I know you've met Caterina Savona, Riccardo, but I don't believe you've met Caterina Scuderi."

Rick shook his head and laughed. "Well, well. Captain Scuderi, it is indeed a pleasure." He gave her a short bow. "I've heard so much about you, and finally we meet."

"You can still call me Caterina, Riccardo. Come sit." She patted the cushion next to her. Rick sat, and Betta took the place on his right.

"A thorn between roses," Rick said.

"Let me get you a glass of wine, Riccardo." Innocenti walked to a table and filled a glass without waiting for a reply. He passed it to Rick and then raised his own. "To the recovery of the missing Jacopos." Rick clinked his glass with those of the two Innocenti and then with Caterina's. Her face showed nothing.

"And may they never be lost again," Innocenti added, after they all sipped the red wine. He took a seat. "Caterina has told us that they have been found, Riccardo, but hasn't given any details. She must be finding it difficult to get out of her mysterious undercover role." They all waited for Captain Scuderi to respond.

"It will all come out in due time," she said. "You know how bureaucracies work, and the ministry is no different. Procedures must be followed at all cost."

"Not even a hint?" asked Betta, leaning forward to ask the question across Rick.

"We must allow Caterina to deal with the ministry," Rick said quickly. "I'm sure it will become public soon enough, probably with a press conference involving the higher-ups."

"The important thing is that they've been found." Caterina spoke in a tone that attempted to end the discussion. "Why don't we go to dinner?"

Betta bounced to her feet. "I haven't had time to change, with the surprise of meeting the new Caterina. I won't be long." She slipped out the door into the hallway under Rick's gaze.

"And I really should put on a different shirt. May I leave my guests alone? Help yourself to the wine." Innocenti disappeared through a door.

Rick got to his feet, picked up the bottle from the table, and held it up for Caterina. She shook her head and he splashed a bit into his own glass. "You talked to Beppo."

"He called me right after he spoke with you."

Rick sat where Innocenti had been, across from her. "I sense that you don't agree."

She straightened her skirt and leaned back against the leather cushions. "The ministry's reward money is meant for people who have helped find lost art, not for those who have knowingly broken the law by keeping stolen works in their possession."

"You never met Professor Gaddi."

Caterina looked up at Rick and tilted her head slightly. "I will now, since I'll be setting up his reward payment." The way she emphasized the word "reward" left no doubt as to how she felt. "Would it make a difference if I'd met him?"

"I suppose not." He took a drink and thought that her annoyance may be due to not being the one to track down the missing Jacopos. Better not to ask. "Are you going to fight this?"

She smiled. "No, Riccardo. Remember the running path in the park? Let's say I'm returning the favor."

"That wire was meant for me, you know."

"It doesn't matter. You saved me from serious injury or worse. But to be honest, there's something else." She picked up the paper napkin from under her glass and patted her smiling lips. "Your friend Beppo knows too many people for me to get on his wrong side."

◇◇◇

Betta snuggled her head under Rick's chin. "Does it bother you that you were wrong?"

His brow furrowed. "About what?"

"You were sure the murder was connected to the two missing Jacopo paintings."

"It was about two paintings, only they weren't by Jacopo Bassano. So I was half right." He took a sniff of her hair. "Betta, I've been trying to identify your perfume and now it's finally come to me. Dahlia Noir, am I correct? Givenchy?"

"You really pride yourself on knowing perfumes, don't you?"

"It's important."

"And you couldn't quite remember this one."

"I knew I would eventually."

"Perhaps you remembered when you saw the bottle on my dresser?"

Rick body stiffened. "Betta, I'm shocked that you would even—"

"A thousand pardons, Riccardo, that I would even think of accusing you of deception."

He pulled her closer, if that was possible. "By the way, why don't you call me Rick. It's shorter, easier to write in e-mails when I'm back to Rome."

"*Va bene*, Rick." She pronounced it "reek," but he didn't correct her. "Though it may not be necessary to write e-mails."

"Because we'll be talking so often on the phone?"

"It's not what I meant. I was talking with Caterina before you arrived, and she says they need more women with the art cops and she'd be happy to put in a good word for me. And then there's your good friend Beppo. Does he have much influence?"

He took in another whiff of her perfume. "When would your training start?"

Chapter Fifteen

Commissario Piero Fontana pulled the white napkin from his collar, revealing the striped tie that his nephew had brought back for him from Bassano del Grappa. The silk went perfectly with the white shirt and dark blue suit, causing Rick to wonder if the man had actually gone out and bought a suit to match a new tie. He wouldn't put it past his uncle. The napkin had been necessary for their first course, *spaghetti alle vongole*. The small, *veraci* clamshells now formed stacks on dishes next to their empty pasta bowls. Well, almost empty. Rick still had a few strands of spaghetti which would not go to waste, nor would the garlic-flavored olive oil that coated them. He reached for another piece of bread while his uncle filled their glasses. The Frascati was nearly achromatic, but what it lacked in hue it made up for in body.

"It is unfortunate, Riccardo, that you had to suffer through an encounter with Giuliano Occasio. It is a sad truth that there are many such men in the ranks of the *Polizia di Stato*. I was going to intervene on your behalf, but…" He raised a hand when he saw Rick was about to interrupt. "My dear nephew, I was contacted early on by Detective DiMaio. Did you really believe he would not keep his old instructor informed?"

"I didn't think about it."

"He didn't tell you because I asked him not to. After he called I expected to hear from you and when I didn't, I must admit I was surprised. And somewhat disappointed. But after thinking more about it, I've concluded that it was the right thing for you not to have brought your uncle in on this one. It is the American coming out in you, of course, the influence of your footwear." He chuckled. "But in my opinion, which I admit is biased, it demonstrates again that you have missed your true calling."

Rick shook his head. "*Zio*, let's not start on that again."

"Your friend Betta is using her connections to secure a position in the art police, you could certainly—"

"I'm perfectly happy doing what I'm doing. You know that."

Piero sighed and picked up his wineglass. "*Purtroppo,* I do know that, but you must forgive me for trying anyway. Don't tell my sister that I have again attempted to push you into law enforcement."

"What happens in Roma stays in Roma, *Zio.*"

"Excellent. Regarding DiMaio, I have already, as you requested, spoken with the right people. He will not be disappointed with his new assignment."

"He will be most appreciative, as am I."

The commissario waved off the comment with his hand. "It is how things work, and I am glad to help. I remember DiMaio, he is the type of officer that should be helped, and not only because he befriended my nephew."

Rick had been wondering if the befriending was due mainly to his having an uncle in the high echelons of the police, but he kept the thought to himself. Piero continued.

"Now you must tell me about this young lady. I assume she is attractive?"

"Most attractive, *Zio.* I look forward to your meeting her."

"As do I. I'm surprised that she in fact wished to come to Rome. Normally the women you meet take the first opportunity to get on an airplane for America."

"Ouch."

"Sorry, Nephew, I could not resist. And *la bella* Erica, did she make the right decision?"

They watched as one waiter picked up their plates and another positioned menus in their place. Rick took a drink from his wineglass. "I've stopped trying to understand Erica. Time will tell if she's done the right thing, and even if she has, that doesn't mean the marriage will endure. If she truly wants it to work, I think it will."

Piero put on his half glasses and they both studied the menus for a full minute. The decision on the second course loomed. Rick put his down and looked at his uncle. "Did you ever actually work with Inspector Occasio, *Zio?*"

The older man gave the question some thought. "No. Fortunately the police force is large enough so that we were never in the same *questura*. My encounter with him, if that is the correct word, was indirect. A man from his hometown was working for me on a corruption investigation. It was when I was assigned to Bari, though the place is irrelevant. This man got too close to various people involved in the investigation. I suspected that he was being bribed and had tampered with the evidence, though I wasn't able to prove it. But I did pull him off the case and had him reassigned to another part of the country. Occasio heard about it and tried to get me to smooth things over, and when I wouldn't, he tried to discredit me. He went behind my back, of course, though I heard about it from others. The man he was trying to protect was eventually fired from the force when he got into trouble somewhere else."

"Despite your being proven right, Occasio hasn't forgiven you."

"Those types never do."

"So Detective DiMaio's advice not to tell him you were my uncle was sound."

Piero continued to study the menu. "It's impossible to know what Occasio would have done to Commissario Fontana's *nipote*, if anything. But I doubt it would have improved your relationship with the man." He put down the menu. "I think I'm going to order the *vitello al limone*."

The veal also sounded good to Rick, but he decided to have his cutlet breaded. It would be thin and served with a lemon wedge and nothing else, unlike the chicken fried steak with gravy and mashed potatoes he used to devour at a favorite restaurant in Albuquerque. The waiter appeared an instant after Piero turned his head slightly toward the kitchen, and they made their requests.

Rick noticed the look on his uncle's face and knew from experience that something profound was in the offing. It was usually at this point in the meal that any serious issues were brought to the table. He couldn't think what it might be. Piero had been studying a spot on the tablecloth, and now his eyes rose and met Rick's.

"Riccardo, this arrangement you made with Beppo to get the reward money for Professor Gaddi—"

"The art cops have very large resources for such things."

"I'm sure they do, but that is not what concerns me. You misrepresented what really happened. Gaddi understood perfectly what he'd been doing, and had known it for years. I'm certain that the regulations are quite clear on how those funds are to be used, apart from the law itself about stolen goods. Between the two…" His words stopped. The point had been made.

Rick looked squarely at his uncle. "The man needed help, not prosecution."

Commissario Fontana took off his glasses and folded them carefully into his jacket pocket. His hand rubbed along the side of his chin as if deciding whether the short beard needed a trim.

Rick watched and waited.

After a long silence, Piero raised a hand to signal the waiter. "We will need a new wine to go with our second courses, Riccardo."

Author's Note

Bassano del Grappa, like the settings for my other books, is an Italian city that doesn't get the tourist recognition it deserves. It normally sits quietly on its hill at the base of the Alps watching the tourists stream by on their way to nearby Venice and other more famous cities in the Veneto region. Which is a shame, because it is a place with much to offer. Its charms begin with the covered Ponte degli Alpini, featured on the cover of this book. It was designed by the most famous of Italian architects, Andrea Palladio, and has been associated for decades with the Italian alpine troops. The bridge, which has been destroyed and rebuilt numerous times over the centuries, now is the accepted symbol of the city.

But there are other gems to draw a visitor to this town. The ceramics museum in Palazzo Sturm tells the story of the industry that has been centered in Bassano for centuries. A glazed pumpkin in our kitchen is evidence that ceramics artisans continue to thrive there. The Castello Superiore, a walled bastion at the highest point in the city, dates to Roman times and encloses the ancient Duomo along with other stone structures. Down from the castle, on one of Bassano's beautiful plazas, sits the San Francesco church, attached to the former convent that is now the Museo Civico, the pride of the city. It is there that one finds the world's finest collection of paintings by Jacopo da Bassano, also called Jacopo Ponte. The two paintings by Jacopo that are a key part of this book's story do not exist, of course, but his work and legacy most definitely do. Back in the day, his neighbors must have wondered how they were going to keep Jacopo down in Bassano after he's seen Venice, but he confounded them by remaining loyally planted to his roots. If for nothing else, you've got to admire the man for that.

Two towns near Bassano are the background for scenes in the book. Marostica, to the west, is famous for its annual live chess match and the walls which meander up and down the hill behind it. Cittadella is a town with an imposing circular wall system, its internal streets forming concentric circles inside the ramparts. It was built as a military response by Padova to Castelfranco Veneto, a walled town put up just to the east by the Venetians. So for a while they faced off each other across the border between the two city-states. Both are well worth visiting. There is a mention of Asolo, just east of Bassano, but Rick doesn't manage to get up there. This tiny village is a true jewel, sitting in a place of honor above the plain. If you can't get to Asolo, you might stop by, of all places, Sarasota, Florida. There you'll find the eighteenth-century Asolo Theater, whose decorative interior was transported from an Italian warehouse in 1949 and beautifully restored inside a new building on the grounds of the Ringling Museum.

Thanks go to my son, Max, for his expertise in things mechanical, this time motorcycles. And once again my wife, Mary, came up with great ideas to fix things whenever the story got into a bind, and helped to keep my descriptions accurate. She also knows her perfume.

To receive a free catalog of Poisoned Pen Press titles, please provide your name and address in one of the following ways:

Phone: 1-800-421-3976
Facsimile: 1-480-949-1707
E-mail: info@poisonedpenpress.com
Website: www.poisonedpenpress.com

Poisoned Pen Press
6962 E. First Ave. Ste 103
Scottsdale, AZ 85251